The Nuns of Baboob

Book One of the Sultanate of Baboob Chronicles

CD Damitio

Vagobond Books
2026

ISBN: TBD — enter before KDP upload

Published by Vagobond Books

indignified.com/books

Series: Book One of the Sultanate of Baboob Chronicles

First Edition, 2026

To all of those who are on a journey to Baboob.

Contents

Dipshit

Martin Hutchins was a lovable douchebag. Affectionately called "Dipshit" by those who knew and loved him (even his mom) and called Martin only by people who didn't know him and read his name from documents. He was a man approaching middle-age who women found handsome: in an 'if he were thinner, if he were taller, if he had more hair, if he weren't so neurotic,' but maybe 'just for the weekend' kind of way. He remained a personification of the 'high school loser' well past high school. He was a thirty-five-year-old college student who had never left Las Vegas and never had a job that wasn't funded by a casino in one way or another.

We need to set a few things straight about this story before we go any further. This story is not about Martin Hutchins, though he is a convenient vehicle for telling it. This story is (as the title specifies) about the nuns of Baboob. If you haven't heard of the nuns of Baboob or the Sultanate of Baboob, don't worry. You're not alone. That's the reason this story is so important.

We do however, need to tell you about Martin in order to introduce you to the nuns of Baboob. Too many things about Martin, if you ask me, way too many things. Martin's love life consisted of one night stands with drunk women who firmly believed what happens in Vegas, stays in Vegas – especially when he was what happened. He never managed have a romantic relationship that lasted longer than a few days until he met me...and for those who say that he had a longer relationship with a certain royal slut, that doesn't count. I get to determine that, not you — so just shut up. I'm the narrator and that's all you need to know about me for now. You'll meet me soon enough. Back to Pig...err...Martin...

He didn't believe he was a loser. The same as evil dictators may not think they are monsters but without all the dead bodies. What you believe about yourself is important, but... and this is a huge but, only a douchebag would take out student loans to support his Vegas lifestyle while majoring in “Historical Remembrance and Narco-Linguistic Retention.” With a degree in HR & NLR, Martin could expect to work in a casino until he died just to pay back just the interest on his student loans. His degree from UNLV qualified him for nothing. Not surprising.

This story revolves *around* but isn't *about* Martin. That’s why it’s important to learn how he stopped being 'Dipshit’ Martin Hutchins and why everyone began to call him Pig. Without that moment, there would be no way to tell you about the history, customs, and culture of the Sultanate of Baboob.

Pig

It was 5 a.m. and Martin was as happy as his soon to be namesake in a puddle of shit. He'd graduated from college. He'd won $5000 on the craps table. When he was stumbling out the rotating glass door of the Mirage Casino, a big white limo pulled up to the curb next to him. An older and not very pretty (okay, some people might think she was pretty...or maybe even beautiful but trust me she was slutty) woman in too much makeup opened the door and motioned to him with a curled index finger,

"Come fuck me, Pigrone," she said in a thick Italian accent.

Martin had no willpower to disobey. It wasn't in his nature, no one had ever taught him to avoid slutty older women in big white limousines. Instead, he got in the limo and instantly adopted the name, Pigrone (pronounced peeg-roh-neh), as his own. For a half hour he did unspeakable things with the trashy old Italian lady (who, by the way, was as nameless to Pig as she is to you). She, if we're being honest, fucked his brains out while screaming things that no one should have to think about.

"Oh, Pigrone"

"Yes, Pigrone, YEEESSSS!"

"Defile me, Pigrone."

She dumped him off at the International House of Pancakes. When he asked for her number she laughed.

"What happens in Vegas, stays in Vegas, Pigrone."

Her driver, drove her away.

Torn between exhilaration and disappointment, he settled for a stack of blueberry pancakes to go with the fat stack of cash he had won earlier, still tucked in his jean shorts pocket.

The waitress smiled at him, hoping for a big tip. "What's your name, Hun?" she asked in a fake southern accent.

"Pigrone" he told her, since he liked the breathy sound of it.

She had once taken an Italian class at Pahrump Community College and even though *he* didn't know, *she* knew he had just told her his name was Pig. She left to place his order and decided not to waste any further smiles or conversation on him.

Two coked-out guys in the next booth having a loud conversation over untouched plates of eggs and ham. People are reborn as cartoon characters of themselves when they spend too much time in Las Vegas and these two were a great example. Back in California they were very successful guys with tech jobs but after a weekend in Vegas, both gestured wildly as they spoke. They could sense their own growing irrelevance as middle-aged white men. In a desperate attempt to add importance to the bullshit they were spouting, they used exaggerated gestures and loud voices to prop up their delicate space-Karen egos. Their shirts were unbuttoned to their navels.

"I'm telling you, Sergey, Baboob is going to explode. I heard about it from this genius developer with the most unfortunate name ever," the sandy haired dork laughed as he spoke to the dark haired geek. His expensive jacket and the colorful 'G' monogrammed pocket protector marked him them both as Silicon Valley nerds who had come to Vegas for the whores and coke they could no longer indulge in at their own headquarters. He made loud explosion noises and used his hands to demonstrate landmines going off.

"What was his unfortunate name?" the other tech-bro asked.

"Ted Kazinsky...." They were both laughing and making bomb noises now.

"Wait, you know the Unabomber?" Sergey asked him between bouts of laughter.

"No. Different guy. How fucked up is that? The Ted Kazinsky who isn't the Unabomber."

"I'm not sure I'd listen to a guy with the same name as the Unabomber about anything though."

"Nah, he's a genius. I'd never hire him...because the last thing I want is to have someone think the Unabomber works for us, but seriously, he's Ted Kazinsky is a genius. Both of them. And guess what, he's right, Baboob is going to have insane development and whoever goes there first is going to make a fortune. There are deposits of oil, coal, shale, diamonds, and rubies under Baboob. It's going to be a money shot once their Sultan allows internationals to come in. He's definitely the richest man in the world. Everyone knows but no one can prove it."

Pigrone was listening, but Sergey wasn't.

Sergey's mind took a coke-fueled tangent. It had nothing to do with Baboob or minerals.

"I should have taken a job teaching in Spain after college, Larry. I could have been working in a cool foreign country filled with easy chicks. That sounds so much better than having to worry that everyone was after my money. I'm miserable." Sergey dropped his head into his arm in despair while massaging his barely concealed man-breasts. "I'm wasting my time in Mountain View. All those stuck-up lesbian bitches from the coast only want me for my money."

Pig's stack of blueberry pancakes arrived and he stopped paying attention. He imagined a new future for himself while he poured blueberry syrup on blueberry pancakes. Pigrone Martin – it had a great sound — romantic and exotic. Martin Hutchins was dead. He was Pigrone Martin – adventurer, lover, and international man of mystery! Blueberry Pancakes had never tasted so good!

Over the next two weeks Pigrone redefined himself.

He quit his job at the casino and enrolled in a 'Teaching English as a Foreign Language' course in Spain. He bought a plane ticket to Madrid, made plans to move out of his mom's trailer, and told everyone (including his mom) they had to call him Pigrone instead of Dipshit.

"I'm not sure Pigrone is much better, Dipshit," his mother told him. She had once dated a minor gangster from Sicily and she was pretty sure that she knew what Pigrone meant. The gangster, Vinnie Abufasil, had disappeared when she told him she was pregnant, but there was no guarantee he had been the father. Marvin Hutchins had been happy to claim the child as his own. He had been a pretty great husband until he realized that claiming a child and taking care of a baby were two different things. He'd run off with a girl from Iowa when little 'Dipshit' was three. She didn't mind, he'd been a boring lover. She still dreamed of Vinnie.

Pig wouldn't be dissuaded from his new name, however, and it did seem to be making him happier. She was glad he was leaving.

"You should look for your father in Sicily," she said in an offhand way. Pig briefly wondered what Marvin Hutchins might be doing in Sicily, but then forgot about it.

On the day of his departure, his three friends showed up at the airport with his mother. She had made a giant goodbye banner and they all held it up, waving him off. As he got on the plane they stood at the gate next to the tarmac and unfurled it for all to see. "HASTA LA VISTA DIPSHIT-PIG!!"

He might have been bothered by it on any other day, but today was special. He was leaving Las Vegas for the first time. He was also having his first herpes outbreak — which is a great reason to be wary of drunken Italian women making index finger gestures in casino parking lots at 5 a.m.

The Fucked Five

During his life (spent completely in Las Vegas), when Pig heard the word 'expats' he imagined cool, exotic people. Expats were noble, interesting, and fearless. Beautiful women, adventurous men, and open-minded, intelligent people who didn't fit into their home countries. In his imagination, it was as if one country was not large enough for these noble souls. Expats were his heroes.

He was disappointed with the first expats he met; his classmates at I.S.H.I.T.E.F.L which was an impossibly long abbreviation for the International School for Highly Intensive Teaching English as a Foreign Language. Students since forever had shortened the name to ISHIT. His classmates were mostly Americans in their early twenties who graduated from college during the great recession. They couldn't find work, so they enrolled in the cheapest TEFL course they could find in the hope of finding a way to pay back their student loans. The same thing Pig was doing. They were like him, but very different.

For example, Pig had brought his Indiana Jones hat with him to Madrid and was in his mid-thirties. His classmates had brought fancy clothing for Madrid's nightlife and were mostly in their twenties. The gorgeous Latinas he'd expected to meet in class turned out to be the same trust-fund bitches and self-entitled pricks who had made his life miserable in hight school and college. He was a decade older than most of them and because of that, he was ghettoed with the other four members of his class who weren't in their 20's. Pig dubbed the group, 'The Fucked Five,' though he didn't mention the name to anyone else. Pig amused himself by thinking of them as a terrible band that never made it. The Fucked Five were Margot, Jenny, Bob and Bing — and of course Pig was the lead singer.

Bob and Bing were British men in their 50's. They'd worked in waste disposal until the early 2000s when Bing persuaded Bob to take a vacation to Thailand without their wives. They were trash men in every sense of the word. They returned home with gold chains, deep tans, syphilis, and a desire to never to work or live in England again. Within months, both were divorced and enrolled at ISHIT so they could go back to Thailand, have sex with more teenagers, and keep living a shithead lifestyle. Madrid was a stopping point for them on their way back to what they constantly referred to as 'the good life.'

"I'm Pigrone. I'm from Las Vegas, Nevada," he said to the two British men when they first met. He wasn't great at making friends, but he was willing to try.

Bob and Bing simultaneously tried to fist bump his extended hand and said "Nice to meet you, Pig."

Pig sighed. No one was willing to say his name the way he wanted them to.

Of the four, the only one Pig actually liked was Margot. She was sixty-five and while *he* wasn't sure why he liked her it was really pretty simple. Pig had never had an actual mother figure. His mother sucked. Literally, figuratively pejoratively. In every way a mother could suck, she did. Margot, on the other hand, was that type of older lady who treats everyone like her own kids, and she was a perfect mother. She left Toledo, Ohio when her husband passed away. Her children were grown and had families of their own and she had never had the chance to really explore the world the way she wanted. It was wonderful. After traveling around Europe via a series of 'Rick Steves Tours', she had enrolled in ISHIT so she could further enjoy the museums and climate of sunny Madrid while supplementing her social security with an income. She didn't particularly want to teach. She only wanted a reason to stay longer in Madrid.

The final member of The Fucked Five was Jenny. She was 49, so the closest to Pig's own age but there was something terribly off about her.

"I'm getting a TEFL certificate so I can move to an African nation and help orphans," she told them on the first day of class.

That would have been noble even if a bit odd, except she went on. "I tried to adopt orphans in San Francisco, but I've been rejected because I take anti-depressants and don't have a husband, as if having some son-of-a-bitch sleeping with me would make me a better parent.

Those off-kilter cunts Madonna and Angelina Jolie — no one tells them no. It's not like I don't have a shrink." Realizing she may have gone too far, she smiled sweetly "So I've decided to create my own orphanage but first, ISHIT."

It would be a running joke among the younger members of the class for the duration of their time together. They would speak some outlandish dream like "I'm going to end world hunger...," and then follow it up with "...but first I shit." The majority of them were just trying to avoid getting jobs or starting their real life for a while — this was the equivalent of a gap year. They hoped to spend a year teaching abroad before getting jobs they actually wanted back where they really wanted to be.

On the first day, the instructor asked the class to tell where they were from and where they had traveled. Bob and Bing talked about Thailand. Margot described her adventures in Southern Europe. Jenny talked about time she had spent in Mexico and South America. The younger classmates all seemed to have done a lot of travel before coming to ISHIT. Pig had vast experience with international people in Las Vegas, but he had never been out of Nevada before flying to Madrid. When his turn came he felt ashamed of his limited knowledge. That's why he lied.

Sort of. When they asked where he had been he told them about places he really had been — but in a way that wasn't exactly true.

"I've seen the world," he told them. He was thinking of all the people who come to Las Vegas, all the famous landmarks based on other places within Vegas, and the many nights he spent watching the National Geographic Channel while he was growing up.

"What's the coolest landmark you've visited?" one of the cute young girls asked.

Pig was quick with a true but not true answer. "I love the view from the top of the Eiffel Tower. Paris is wonderful." She had no idea he meant the Paris Casino on the Vegas strip and the slightly smaller version of the Eiffel Tower casino money had built there.

"I used to work in a palace," he said. "I've spent many hours enjoying the wonderful architecture and canals of Venice. No trip is complete without a trip Caesar's Palace and the amazing works of art there."

For of course, one can see the world without leaving Vegas. Sort of.

During a break, Bing sidled up to him and asked "Do you have a fag?"

Images of Bing and Bob with young Thai boys flashed through his head and curdled his stomach as Pig looked at greasy Bing with confusion. He'd asked it so casually. As if he expected the answer to be yes. There were a large number of transsexual prostitutes who walked the streets outside of ISHIT. Pig wondered if Bing was talking about them. He looked at Bing with confusion.

"A fag," Bing made a smoking gesture with his hand going to his mouth "Do you have a smoke?" It was a relief, but if we're being honest, Pig was a bit disappointed. He casually offered Bing a smoke while all these thoughts banged around in his head.

In the lone smoking area, Pig quickly learned that Bing and Bob were the worst kind of humans. Bob told him about a fourteen-year-old prostitute he'd paid $100 to deflower and how important it was to teach 'the young ones' how to enjoy their work. Pig wanted to vomit. He hated them but he didn't have the will to quit smoking nor the will to tell them they were the actual pigs, so he smoked and he listened. He wanted nothing to do with them, but there was only one area where they could smoke at ISHIT — even though the rest of Spain was filled with smokers who smoked everywhere.

There was no stopping Bing or Bob from their disgusting stories. Pig wondered what kind of teachers they were going to be. He hoped the schools did background checks or had safety features built in because he could see these guys harming children. He decided to play the part of a secret agent. He would gather as much information about them as he could and then report them to whatever country they were heading to.

Pig grew up in Vegas, so he knew that the world was filled with deviants but he had never met two as disgusting as Bing and Bob. Too often, he found himself smoking and listening in as the two regaled one another with stories of picking whores from fishbowl rooms and 'breaking in' the new girls. The notebook he put notes about them in became such a dark document that he wanted to burn it.

"You're always here listening, Mate, " Bob said to him "You must have some stories of your own....let's hear one."

He told the story of the Italian woman and how she had named him and given him herpes. They laughed at him. It was decidedly not with him.

"Mate, you've got to wear a glove. No glove, no love," Bob shouted. He gave Bing a high-five.

"Roll it on before you plug it in," Bing responded with another high-five.

Pig felt his ass beginning to itch which meant another herpes outbreak would be coming soon. He hated Madrid and he hated his classmates, especially Bob and Bing. He hated his new life. It was worse than his life in Vegas had been although at least no one called him Dipshit anymore. Pig was a big improvement.

Sexy Nuns

Pig learned some surprising things about himself in Madrid. He discovered that he too, was a sexual deviant. His desires were far less offensive than most but seemingly impossible for him to indulge, though not illegal except maybe in the eyes of God and the church.

He was sexually attracted to nuns. In Vegas he'd seen sexy strippers dressed as nuns. He'd always enjoyed stripping nuns but he'd known they were strippers, not women devoted to God. Madrid was a great place for self discovery about such a thing

In Madrid, he sometimes encountered nuns. In the markets, on the buses, on the train. It didn't matter if they were old or young, he felt a stirring in his loins that could only be attributed to the habits. Pig wasn't sure what to do with that. The fact 'sexy nun' costumes existed meant that he wasn't alone, but he had never considered that he might be attracted to real nuns. There were no real nuns in Las Vegas that he had seen. At least, he had assumed all the nuns he saw in Vegas were the 'sexy nun' variety of prostitute or stripper. Why else would a nun be in Sin City?

Many of the real Madrid nuns were younger, wore tight fitting habits, and seemed to put on the tiniest bit of makeup. Even when he saw ancient nuns he would imagine the hot, young ones which led to a fusion of his memories of 'stripper nuns' superimposed over the actual Spanish nuns. It was complicated and confusing.

There is a significant problem with having a sexual attraction to nuns. Nuns are chaste. They are the Brides of Christ. They are sworn to celibacy. The odds of him finding an actual naughty nun were unlikely at best. He was left with nun-strippers and nun-porn was a popular Spanish niche. He discovered that while surfing Spanish porn sites one night in his apartment.

Pig wanted to fall in love. That was all he'd ever wanted. He'd never had the chance. Now, his chances were even slimmer because he'd fallen in love with the idea of falling in love with a nun who was already in love with God. The idea of having a nun choose him over God felt impossible but he clung to it.

Even someone as prone to fantasy as Pig could see it was not very likely to happen. Anyone else might have said it was impossible, but he wasn't the type to give up on his dreams so easily.

The Cock Bar

If you're reading this in the hope of learning about Madrid or Spain, you are reading the wrong narrative. The most Pig saw of Madrid was a disturbingly named pub called The Cock Bar. It was a quiet place where he could read during breaks. It was the name which first led Margot and Jenny to it, but the next day they mentioned what a disappointment it had been. It was a quiet and dull bar. To Pig, it sounded like the perfect place to relax, smoke, and get away from Bob and Bing. They wouldn't be caught dead going to a place called The Cock Bar — at least not during daylight hours.

The Cock Bar had comfy chairs and cheap drinks. There was even a Spanish slot machine to make him feel at home. It felt more like an English style pub than a Madrid bar, but perhaps that was the reason he liked it. Pig found the desire to be a writer as he walked into The Cock Bar. In fact, the bar had been a focal point for Madrid's literary residents since it opened in 1921, but Pig didn't know that.

Pig didn't make friends with any Spaniards while he was in Spain — except one. Julian and Pig became friends through misunderstanding. Pig didn't realize Julian was the bartender since Julian was sitting on one of the barstools watching soccer on the TV.

"Holá Señor. You like the Cock?" Julian asked while motioning at his dong.

"I'm not interested, thanks," Pig said, thinking perhaps he had come to a gay bar after all.

"No Señor, my bar, The Cock Bar. How do you like The Cock Bar?" Julian often had the same reaction from Americans and he enjoyed it. It was why he motioned at his dong. "My name is Julian, I'm the bartender here."

"Oh, right. Holá Hoolian. Hey, do you spell that with an 'H' or a 'W-H-'?" Pig knew when you show interest in people's names it can endear them to you. His mother had told him.

"Spell what, Señor?" Now it was Julian who was confused.

"Your name. You said it was Hoolian? Right? I've never heard it before. It's interesting." Pig decided the man might be crazy.

"Oh, Señor. Ha ha ha. Hooo-lian. With a J. Just like José Cuervo. Do you see? And what is your name?" Julian was about the same age as Pig but thinner, taller, had more hair, was better looking, and didn't suffer from low self esteem or too many delusions like Pig did. He was the kind of guy who everyone liked right away and because of that, he didn't like anyone very much. He did, however find himself warming to Pig.

"Oh...Jew-lian. I see." And once he knew Julian's name began with a J it became impossible for him to say the name correctly ever again. He held out his hand. "Hi Julian. I'm Pigrone Martin."

Julian was annoyed but at the same time had the unlikely desire to befriend this man. "Señor Pigrone Martin. It's also an interesting name. Are you Italian?"

Pig didn't know what his background was. "I'm American," he said. "Do I look Italian?"

Julian laughed. "Perhaps a little. I'm not sure what you look like, but your name...surely there is a story behind it. I've never met anyone with that name before. Do you know what it means?"

Pig had no idea. It had never occurred to him to think it might have a meaning. Julian could see from the look on Pig's face that he had no idea so he explained.

"It's an Italian word that means lazy. It comes from pigs, but don't worry my friend Pig. In Spain, we love pigs almost as much as we love women. We will eat some together. Let me go get you some jambon." Julian walked behind the bar leaving Pig puzzled. Lazy? Why had she called him lazy?

Julian pull down a dried leg of a pig from where it hung with many others behind the bar. He placed it lovingly on a special rack designed specifically for carving thin slices off of smoked pig legs. With loving precision, he shave the jambon off in almost see through slices, which landed on the hardwood cutting board underneath. He scooped the meat onto a plate and poured two beers from the tap before coming back around the bar again. At 4 p.m. on a Sunday, Pig was the only customer in The Cock Bar.

"Here you are Pig. Can I call you Pig?" Without waiting for an answer, Julian sat down next to him and put the plate on the bar. "Jambon for Señor Pig. Ha ha ha. So, my friend, what brings you to Madrid? Are you here for work or is your mission top secret?"

Pig eyed the man warily but saw no malice in his eyes. Instead he saw warm friendliness. Pig decided to act on this overture of friendship.

"I'm here for a TEFL course. I'm enrolled in ISHIT over near Paseo del Prado. It's a two week intensive course and we've finished the first week. One more week and they will give us a list of the English schools in the country we choose to teach in."

"Señor Pig, of course you will stay in Spain, no?" Julian was looking at him intently.

Pig wasn't sure how to answer. If he answered yes would he be affirming the negative? If he answered no, would he be denying the 'of course'? So he said nothing. Julian fidgeted along the tabletop waiting for an answer. None came.

"Señor, I can see I've asked a question you would prefer not to answer. Perhaps you would rather I mind my own business." Julian stood up.

"No, no. It's not that..." Pig felt like he was losing his only friend, even though they had just met. "I love Spain, but there is a problem. You see..." Pig paused, he wondered if he should tell the truth. He'd only recently admitted it to himself, after all. He was sure Julian would laugh at him. Who wouldn't? He could feel himself blushing.

"Si, my friend. Go on. I think I am starting to understand. This is a matter of love, is it not?" Julian had been a bartender for too long not to recognize the signs of embarrassed love when he saw them. He was certain some Señorita in Madrid had already stolen and crushed his new friend's heart. The women of Madrid could be so incredibly cruel. But, of course, he was wrong.

"Yes," Pig told him, amazed Julian had already seen through him. "That's it exactly. It's a matter of love. I want..."

"Si, Señor Pig. Go on. What is her name? Where did you meet her?" Like all Spaniards, Julian was a romantic. He came from generations of romantics who sang songs of devotion to women every day of the week and then asked for forgiveness for betraying those he had sworn to love each Sunday before meeting another woman he would swear to love again. “Yes, I understand. These women in Madrid.”

“No. I mean yes, it is the women of Madrid, sort of I mean. It's a little complicated, I'm embarrassed...” Julian understood immediately.

“My friend, just because you are in love with a man doesn't make you a homosexual. In fact some of the best love I've ever had was...” Julian came from a long line of men who saw no shame in loving another man in whatever way wine and passion saw fit and Pig wasn't the first foreigner he had met who had fallen for the charms of Spanish men and found himself confused about his feelings.

Pig interrupted him before he could go on. “No, I'm not infatuated with a man. It's the nuns. I can't stop thinking about the nuns. I'm obsessed with your Spanish nuns and I want to fall in love with and marry one. I want to spend my life with a nun. ” It all rushed out in a jumble.

Julian understood, he came from a long line of ... “What? Señor, did you say you want to marry a nun?” Julian didn't understand at all. He was Catholic and while he and every other Catholic boy had certainly had sexual fantasies about nuns, he had never heard of anyone wanting to marry one. “Señor, these are the brides of Christ. They cannot marry. It's impossible!”

Julian was trying to put the pieces together. “Pig, have you met a nun who wants to marry you? Have you slept with a nun?” The excitement rising in Julian was part anger at Pig's blasphemy but in larger part due to the fact he was imagining Pig had actually found a nun who would put out. “Señor, where is she?”

“No, no, no,” Pig said. “This is all coming out wrong. There isn't one specific nun. It's all of them. I lust after nuns but with my emotions.....”

Ah, Julian understood. The desire of the veil. The chaste woman hidden from all. The desire for the virgin. Yes, he understood it completely. “Oh, my friend Pig. Yes, I understand. I can tell you this, you will never marry a nun because the moment she gives up her vows she will stop being a nun and you will thirst after her sisters.” Pig had never thought it through. He listened intently as Julian went on.

“Señor Pig, I think we will be friends. There is something about you that makes me want to help you. Tomorrow, I will show you something that will make you forget nuns forever. Tomorrow, you and I will head somewhere special and I will show you the women of your dreams. The nuns of Baboob...but I've said too much already"

Despite Pig's many questions, Julian refused to provide further details about leading him to Pig's own twisted version of paradise. Julian looked at him with those big dark eyes and shook his head no.

"My friend, I'm afraid I can tell you nothing further without causing you to find reasons to destroy something beautiful." Julian came from a long line of philosophers and knew something about human nature, having watched all manner of escapades take place in The Cock Bar. "If I were to tell you more, you would certainly head there without waiting for me to lead you. How could you resist? What man would hold himself back from the woman of his dreams. Mañana, my friend. Tomorrow will come soon enough."

Pig found it frustrating, as he'd always found Christmas frustrating. He didn't like waiting. He didn't like surprises. His imagination created a world that always exceeded the limits of the real world. Anything he thought about for too long inevitably became a disappointment. It was better to know what was coming than to build one's expectations too high. Hope and expectation both led to disappointment for Pig because he always allowed the one to turn to the other.

Julian was not moved by Pig's pleading. He repeated "Mañana" and then, when customers began to come into the bar, when bar maids began to come to him for change, and as Spaniards all over Madrid woke from their afternoon siesta, Julian moved to his trade and profession. Pig would have to wait.

Pig tried one last gambit. "Julian, I've just remembered. I have class tomorrow. I will be at ISHIT all day. Tell me where to go so I can go now."

Julian arched an eyebrow and looked at Pig with what could only be described as disappointment at the feebleness of the attempt. "Señor Pig, my friend, we won't be going during the day. I don't have to work in the Cock tomorrow so I will sleep until 4 or 5 pm. After that, I will wake, eat breakfast, and then you will come meet me here at 8 pm. You will have to save the rest of your questions until then because my Cock has suddenly become very busy."

It was true. Every table and every chair had been filled and there was no longer standing room at the bar. A line of men and women, mostly well-dressed Spaniards, formed at the door as people waited to enjoy the mellow vibe of The Cock Bar. As for Julian, he was moving from one end of the bar to the other, working with the bar maids, telling jokes to men in dark business suits, and still finding time to flirt with the pretty women who managed to squeeze their way to the front of the bar to place their drink orders. His eyes met Pig's and he said one word. “Mañana.”

Nun of Your Business

Tomorrow did come, as it always does. As the day progressed, Pig attempted to keep his mind on learning grammar. It was difficult to focus on what distinguished the passive voice, making comparisons, and the present simple versus the present perfect. Each lesson in grammar seemed to emphasize some lesson he had missed, not in English, but in life.

He had let the passive voice carry him along without truly exerting or making himself heard. He had let life happen to him, rather than being an active participant. He considered the one time in his life he hadn't been passive. Leaving Las Vegas. Beyond that, he had allowed life to pull him along by the balls like a slutty Italian making enticing finger movements.

When it came to making comparisons, he was perpetually miserable through the practice of it. If he threw a perfect pass in a game of touch football, he mentally compared himself with someone who threw two perfect passes, or three passes, or someone that was Joe Montana. In other words, he could never feel good because of his compulsion to create comparisons. It was in life as it was in sport. Someone else always had a better looking girlfriend, someone else was always more handsome, someone else always had a better cell phone.

He watched Bob and Bing fiddling with their iPhones. They talked about getting thicker gold chains when they retuned to Thailand. He realized he wasn't the only one stuck on making comparisons. Perhaps, the reason expats like Bob and Bing became such scumbags was because as expats there was less to compare themselves to. It was something to think about.

Back to grammar where the simple present vs. the present perfect went way beyond the rules of the English language. The simple present was pretty good. Here he was, Pig Martin, sitting in Madrid, attending a class, meeting interesting people, and on his way to something fantastic as soon as this evening. Then, comparisons came in again because rather than be content with that, he couldn't help comparing it to what he imagined would be the present perfect. He would be in Madrid with the love of his life, she would be showing him the incredible architecture and beauty of this amazing city, deep inside the recesses of the cathedral she would pull him into a nave, lift off her habit, and ...

Nuns again. How in the world would Julian show him something better than nuns? What could surpass the present perfect of a horny nun that gave up God for him? But then, as he thought about it — he realized Julian had been right. As soon as she gave up her vows, she was a flawed woman, no longer perfect, no longer clean. He was one sick puppy.

** ** ** ** ** ** **

During the break, Margot invited him to join her and Jenny at the Cava Baja area that evening. They were going to eat tapas, explore the trendy wine bars in the narrow cobbled streets, and try to find a specific area Margot had read about.

"Pigrone, you've got to see these things," Margot said to him. Out of the entire class (the entire world) she was the only one who called him Pigrone instead of Pig. She opened her guidebook and showed him a picture. "These are caves carved into a building and they are filled with flamenco and Spanish guitar. Mesones. They're called Mesones and they are incredible. I remember on the Rick Steves Tour of Madrid they took us there but I think I can find it..."

One of the younger girls in the class overheard the conversation. Open hostility oozed from the younger members of the class towards those who were older. It was as if they resented the intrusion of adults in their youthful world. The girl, a dark haired New York princess named Melody, always wore incredibly expensive clothes and carried an ostentatious Louis Vuitton bag everywhere she went.

"Tourists like those on your Rick Steves' tours who have ruined Madrid and every other European city. You and your group sneak into places where you have no right to be, a big group of blue hairs with too much money and you make the prices go up, you drive out the authentic locals, and before you know it they are putting in wheelchair ramps and parking for tour buses. Why not throw away the guidebook and find something on your own? Or better yet, go back home."

Pig was surprised to hear this coming from this particular girl. She spent every break they had buying things that seemingly got more and more expensive in the nearby shops. She would need to pay for extra baggage space wherever she went. She spoke perfect Spanish and was usually picked up from the dorm apartments by fit and handsome Spaniards. He never saw her come back because he was always asleep well before she and her friends returned. He tried to consider what she was saying, but he couldn't really get past the fact that a nice old lady like Margot shouldn't have to wander around dark streets by herself to find something authentic. This would have been a great chance for him to defend Margot, but when he started to speak, Melody turned and walked away.She was the kind of girl would even notice a passive dipshit like him unless it was so that she could punish herself...

Jenny, who was sitting quietly watching the exchange, exploded. Over the weekend thieves had broken into her dorm and stolen her anti-depressants and Xanex. It might have had something to do with her reaction.

"Get back here, you self-righteous little bitch. Just because your daddy has millions of dollars and you've never had to work in your life doesn't mean we have to listen to your ageist discrimination," Jenny ranted. Jenny's dirty blond hair seemed to be losing a grip along with her. She shook her head like a lion's mane as words and spittle blew out of her mouth in foul streams. "You like to spread your whore legs for every Spanish dick that wants to fuck you, little whore.It doesn't mean you have anything special because you're gonna lose your youth too and then, you pathetic gym sock, you're gonna find men will stop paying for everything and taking care of you and making your life easy and then you're going to have to start really working and no one will let you adopt children and then you'll be really fucked."

Melody smiled condescendingly as she interrupted Jenny with "That sounds like your story...."

Jenny hit her.

It took Bob, Bing, Pig, and Margot to pull Jenny away from her. Bob and Bing had both been exceptionally mellow that day but when

Jenny freaked out, they rushed over looking guilty to help disengage her. Melody went back to her seat muttering “Filthy hag.”

The ISHIT instructor came back and everyone turned to contemplating the past imperfect. At the next break, Pig let the women know that he wouldn't be able to join them that night. Bob and Bing suggested he go to the Chueca neighborhood north of Gran Via with them. They had heard that there were some 'specialist' strip bars around Infantas and Hortaleza and wanted to see if they could find a donkey or banana show. Pig couldn’t turn down their skeezy offer fast enough. The two men wouldn’t shut up with stories of the many things they had seen put in and taken out of vaginas during their time. Pig found it hard to believe that either of them weren’t in jail.

With class over, Pig left ISHIT, took a shower, and made his way to the The Cock Bar. Julian was there waiting for him. All day, Pig had been trying to remember why Julian's mention of Babooban women had tickled his memory but it wasn't until he saw Julian eating a plate of bacon and eggs that he remembered the Larry and Sergey's conversation at the IHOP in Las Vegas. Baboob. The land where oil would gush like a money shot.

Julian hugged Pig like a long lost friend. His kisses on Pig's cheeks were like those for a brother despite the fact that the two men had only met the day before and spoke for no more than an hour. “Mi Amigo Pig, my brother, my friend. I am so happy to see you again. Do you know that I thought you might not come today? I thought you might be the type of man who would refuse to see his dreams come true. The type of man who prefers to wallow — and please excuse the metaphor — in the mud of his own misery, but what am I saying? Of course, I knew you would come, that you are the pig of destiny...”

Pig wasn't sure how to respond to all of that so he said “Oh, yeah, well, yes. Holá , Julian.”

Julian insisted that Pig join him for several beers and some simple tapas. “My friend, where we will go tonight, you will not find any alcohol. I don't know how they do it, but sadly it is true.”

Several beers turned to five and finally at ten o'clock they set out. Julian took them first to the Plaza de Mayo where he told the story of the sweet seamstress Manuela Malasaña who had worked hard for her father and in the midst of the great Peninsula War had been brutally murdered by occupying French troops who saw her scissors as some sort of a dangerous weapon. After this, she had become a martyr to the Spanish cause when the French executed her. The entire area was now called Malasaña in her honor.

"And so, my friend," Julian explained, " I bring you to a place that is where the power of women goes well beyond this life and into the next."

They walked through the tight streets of the neighborhood past bar after bar, Pig couldn't imagine that they wouldn't be able to find alcohol anywhere in this area. There were so many bars. The music streaming into the street was punk, metal, ska, and grunge. Slowly, the number of bars began to decrease.

Pig suddenly remembered Baboob... "Julian, are you taking me to Baboob?"

The Spaniard turned to him and laughed. "Baboob? How, my friend, could I possibly take you to Baboob? Baboob sits in the center of the dark continent, a mysterious country colonized by escaped Arab slaves and smugglers from Andorra – ruled by Em-Mucho, a notorious tyrant, the son of an assassin and a famed Egyptian singer. Baboob – so far away both culturally and geographically...how in the world, my friend, could I be taking you to Baboob?"

Pig felt enthralled with the description and foolish for having asked. He really needed to look at maps more often. He'd been thinking...well never mind what he'd been thinking because Julian wasn't through speaking.

"However, in one sense you are right, my perceptive and wise friend. I am taking you to a piece of Baboob. I am bringing you to the closest thing to Baboob you can find outside of Baboob. Have you noticed the smell?"

Pig hadn't, but he decided to check. Yes, there was a different smell. It was the smell of cinnamon and spices, the smell of grilled meat, the smell of something... He looked around and was surprised to find that the bars were gone. There was not a single bar within sight any longer. The people were different too. Darker, thinner, shorter — it was hard to say how they were different, but they were. A delicious smell caused him to turn to where a woman walked by with a plate of something held on the top of her head. Pig gasped.

The woman was dressed... the way she was dressed. It was like nothing he had ever seen.

He turned to Julian who stood smiling. “Yes, my friend. It is to see the Babooban women we have come here tonight. As you can see, there is something very nun-like about the dress of these women.”

Indeed there was. The Babooban woman wore a cloak, a cowl, and a veil that looked exactly like a nun's habit except that the material was soft and colorful. She looked at Julian and Pig with a flirtatious smile as she went by them.

“Come my friend,” Julian motioned to a tiny shop with tiny tables on which stood tiny cups on tiny saucers. He sat on a tiny stool and motioned for Pig to take the one across from it. With a gesture to the proprietor, a nearly bent-in-half man with the longest beard Pig had ever seen, Julian placed their order.

“Now, Señor Pig, it is time for you to learn the story of Baboob and there is no better place to discover it than here, drinking Master Mucho’s Pickle Spiced tea.”

A Short History of The Sultanate of Baboob

Julian's history of Baboob was both colorful and aromatic, thanks to Master Mucho's Pickle Spiced Tea. However, it will be a disservice to the reader to not give a more fact-filled account of the history of Baboob.

Baboob occupies the interior of several mountainous regions sitting between Libya and Tunisia. It is a decentralized religious monarchy with no contiguous borders. The country itself is one of the smallest in Africa and measures in at only 146 square miles or maybe it's 416 miles, with no borders it's hard to say for sure. In terms of population, Baboob has about 150,000 residents of which nearly half live in the capital city of Turban.

Baboob is ruled by a hereditary sultanate with a line of succession designated by a combination of parentage and *manna*. *Manna* is a measure by the Baoist clergy which determines which heir is the closest to God, using a system which to this day has not been made public. The current ruler is the direct descendent of the first sultan and bears the name Em-Mucho. Residents refer to the ruler as Sultan or Em-Mucho.

Baboob is landlocked and consists mostly of mountains. There is a large river which begins in Tunisia, flows through part of Baboob and then continues into Libya. There is another river that is rumored to run through Baboob, but no one who doesn't live there has ever seen it and those who do live there don't talk about it with outsiders. So that's enough about that. Baboob's official language is Arabic. Most residents also speak French, Italian, or Catalan. There is a sizable minority who speak the native Berber tongue, sometimes called Babooberber. The unit of currency is the Baboobie, called the 'boob' which can be broken down into one-hundred boobies.

The population identifies as 100% Babooban though genetically it can be broken down into the following groups. 47% Arab-Andoran-Babooban 26 % Babooban-Andorran-Italian 13% Arab-Babooban-Italian 11% Andoran-Babooban and 2% Babooban.The last one percent made is made up of 100% Arabs who refuse to be genetically tested. The reason for the low percentages of pure ethnicity is because of the Arab-Andorran wars of 1893-1897 in which those claiming pure blood were nearly wiped out by genocidal tribesmen as a result of a perceived skewing of metrics on the part of the hereditary succession. But that's a completely different story and something this brief history is not going to cover.

Baboob was founded in 1138 AD. The founding of the Sultanate of Baboob began when a group of Tunisian pirates raided the Convent of St. Adelaide which sat in the province of Ragusa on the island of Sicily. They made off with the 150 nuns who had been cloistered there. This was forty years after Sicily had been retaken from the Arabs and the majority of the Norman population there was slain in the battle.

En route back to Tunisia, the pirate fleet encountered a group of Andorran smuggling ships which they attempted to seize. The Andorran fleet proved a tougher target than expected however and killed nearly all of the Arab raiders. Upon boarding the Arab ships, the Andorrans were surprised to find nuns and the wives and children of the Arab raiders.

Needing food and water, the Andorrans put to shore at the Tunisian village of Jargis at which point more Tunisian pirates showed up, burned the ships, and pursued the Andorran smugglers, Sicilian Nuns, and captive Arab women and children into the interior. The Andorran's were skilled mountaineers (as all Andorran smugglers are required to be) and they not only eluded pursuit, but also stumbled upon the isolated valley of Baboob, a land rich in olives, dates, figs, fresh water, and goats.

The chief of the Babooban people welcomed the refugees and offered them his protection if they would all convert to Baoism, the ancient religion. In order to protect the sanctity of his lands he married each of the Andorran men to four Babooban wives. Why four? Generally men are intolerable 75% of the time so the Babooban culture requires each man to have four wives so that the suffering of each woman is reduced. Each man found himself not only a Baoist, but also in the proud possession of four wives.

The Andorrans, not wanting to leave behind the world of royal politics, insisted that the humble chief of the Babooban's be crowned Sultan and since until that day the title for the Sultan is Em-Mucho. Upon reaching adulthood, all the men of Baboob take the name Mucho. It is interesting to note that the Andorran's were also renamed Mucho. To be clear , there is only one Em-Mucho but mucho Muchos.

As for the nuns and the wives and children of the Tunisian pirates (who were quite happy to be away from their pirate husbands), they were all renamed Fatima, as is the custom for all Babooban women when they reach adulthood. As free women, they were allowed to choose their own husbands but they had to marry. There were not enough husbands to go around, but because of the 4:1 rule, soon they were all married. The exotic looks and high status of the nuns led to their clothing being imitated by the native Babooban women. Habits and veils became a part of the traditional costume of the region. The nuns of Baboob are not nuns, but in a sense they are nuns.

Over time, Baboob became a prosperous trading (and smuggling) nation with peculiar customs and a culture and religion like nothing else in North Africa. Because of the high number of wives each man took, they produced a huge number of offspring. Arab traders occasionally took up residence in Baboob and contributed to the culture and genetic heritage as did the children and wives of the Tunisian pirates.

Having become rich nobles, it is easy to see why neither the nuns nor the smugglers chose to return home. Isolation and difficult to navigate mountain passes kept Baboob safe from invasions and tribal warfare throughout much of its history, but in the twentieth century it was its mountainous locations which kept it safe since neither Mohammar Quaddafi of Libya nor Zine El Abidine Ben Ali of Tunisia wanted to risk warfare over a tiny mountain nation that neither country could claim.

Besides, everyone knew that Baboob had the bomb. It never pays to mess with the descendants of smugglers and pirates. As the North African folk saying goes “Al Baboob Makenish Haroob” or “Baboob has no war”. The statement is said when one is saying something obvious much like the North American, “Does a Bear Shit in the Woods?”

Bafia

“And so, my friend, Señor Pig,” Julian's hands continued to gesture as he explained the wonders that walked all around them, “Now you can see that truly there is something better than nuns and you can perhaps hope to find happiness instead of the shame and disappointment you were heading towards.”

Julian paused in his colorful tale of the Babooban Sultanate as Master Mucho brought them another round of Pickle Juice Tea which Julian had already incorrectly explained came from the Andoran love of pickles combined with the Babooban love of tea.

Pig had been taking it all in as he watched the Babooban's around him. Women of all ages with olive complexions, flirtatious eyes, and gloriously colorful habits. Men with long beards, mountain boots, and large knives tucked into their belts.

“There's one thing I don't understand Julian.” Pig finally managed to get out. “Why isn't there any alcohol here? I thought pirates and smugglers loved booze?”

The Spaniard once again looked offended at Pig's lack of knowledge. “Pig, Pig, Pig. There are some things that are the way they are. The Canadian's love of maple syrup, the Spaniards love of pig, the Italian's love of cheese, and for the Baboobans it's the love of God who they call Bao. They are a religious people and the basis of their religion,” he whispered here “is Islam even if they deny it. While they are descended from the brides of Christ, they are the children of Em-Mucho. The major prohibitions of Islam still, mostly, apply to the Babooban people, even if they have walked a different path than the Arabs have taken. But then, who knows? Perhaps the Babooban way is the correct way?”

“Yes,” Pig said. “That makes sense, I mean, sort of. But I still don't understand why there isn't any booze here.” Pig was starting to feel hungry because in truth, the tapas are quite small and only designed to keep you drinking-not fill you up- and it had already been at least two hours since they had left The Cock Bar. “Do you think Master Mucho has any jambon?”

With suddenness that Pig would have thought impossible, but that didn't surprise Julian at all, the nearly bent-in-half figure of Master Mucho of the Pickle Juice Tea was next to Pig with his long white beard flowing over the top of Pig's shoulder and his long silver knife held to Pig's throat. Pig had no idea the man was there and was wondering what that cold feeling on his neck was, while Julian calmed down the angry Babooban with the soothing sounds of his charming Spanish. It was only when Master Mucho took the knife from his throat and smacked him across the back of the head that Pig started to understand. To be fair, the entire incident had only taken a few seconds.

A bead of sweat was rolling down the usually cool looking Julian's face. “My friend, Señor Pig, truly you are innocent in the ways of the world. No, no, no,” Julian held up his hands to stop Pig from making the apology which it hadn't yet occurred to Pig to make and went on. “There are three things that you must remember. It is against the Babooban faith to drink alcohol, to eat pork, or to pay taxes. You see, my friend, one of the biggest insults you can make to a Babooban is to call him a seller of pork. The Babooban male carries the knife to protect his honor, not his person. To Master Mucho, when you asked if he had jambon, you were insulting his family, his faith, and his business. Usually this is a crime that can only be redeemed with blood.”

Pig looked towards Master Mucho of the Pickle Juice who now stood several feet away listening to the two men with a cocked head and an amused smile on his face.

“However,” Julian said and grabbed Pig's head to make sure the man was looking directly into his eyes “I told him that you are new to the ways of Baboob and that you would be willing to take some things to his family in Turban when you go to Baboob. That is the only other way to resolve the Babooban blood feud.”

Pig stopped trying to look towards Master Mucho and now looked straight into the eyes of his friend. “I'm going to...Baboob?” he said uncertainly and then “But wait, I'm not going to Baboob, that's crazy, tell him it was only a mistake and that I don't understand or know about his Babooban way...I can't...”

Julian's right hand came across the table and like those of a lover refusing to hear words of denial from one they were bonded to, his finger came to rest on Pig's fleshy lips. “Shhhh....Shhhhh....I know. Of course, you haven't had time to think about it yet, I understand.” And then the left hand caught Pig across the face with a slap that stunned him into silence. “Don't be an idiot. First of all, the reason there is no war in Baboob is because anyone who has a problem with someone else either kills them or is killed. Second, you have started a blood feud with one of the most dangerous families in all of Spain and this is your only way out. Third, and this is important...are you listening...”

Pig was torn between getting up, hitting Julian back, or listening to the rest of what the man was saying. As he considered the first two points, he saw that the old man's hand had gone back to his knife and the smile was gone from his face. Given the speed with which Master Mucho had been ready to behead him, he decided discretion was certainly the better part of valor. He didn't know if Master Mucho understood English or if he had only understood the slap which still stung his face.

Julian was holding his face and staring deeply into his eyes. “What I am about to say is perhaps the most compelling reason why you need to go to Baboob, my friend Señor Pig. Listen to me and listen carefully – Master Mucho comes from an important family. He has four wives in Spain, four wives in Baboob and more than thirty children. Those thirty children have nearly a hundred children of their own. Most of his grandkids are female.”

Pig’s eyes widened at the thought of having a hundred grandchildren. Julian however misunderstood and thought that perhaps Pig was seeing the light he was attempting to shine on him.”Or have you forgotten the Babooban women, Señor Pig?”

As if on cue, a flock of colorful nun-garbed young women walked by where they were sitting. The curves of their bodies apparent underneath the thin material of their habits and cowls. While their hair was covered, their eyes were a rainbow of blues, greens, browns, and grays while their gentle smiles hid mischievous looks. Oh yes, they were certainly beautiful....

"But," Pig stammered "These aren't nuns, what about the innocence? What about the chastity? I mean, I think it's the forbidden nature of them that I really like, I would imagine that these girls have already..."

Another slap across his face stopped his words. "I had thought you were a man of intelligence, Señor Pig. Do not make the mistake of insulting the honor of the Babooban women. You've already received one reprieve from the executioner tonight. I do not think he will grant you a second."

Master Mucho now came with more pickle juice tea. Perhaps that was the most surprising thing about the evening: the fact that one could actually enjoy tea flavored with pickles. For some reason the fresh dill brought out the delicate flavor of the cucumbers and the splash of vinegar served to make one forget that it was, in fact, pickle juice tea.

The old man stared into Pig's face with a fierce expression and then surprised him with a wink and a gold toothed grin.

Julian continued. "Think about it, Pigrone. These girls are the descendants of nuns and Muslims. They wear these sexy habits and have those flirtatious eyes because they are fishing. A Babooban girl doesn't give away the milk before she sells you the cow. Upon reaching womanhood, all Babooban girls take the nun's vow of celibacy and they become the brides of Bao. Only when they have married are they freed from their vows because in fact, they have married Mucho since all men in Baboob are called Mucho. It is only after the marriage ceremony they lose their earthly virginity. That's how it is supposed to go. You understand?"

Pig's eyes went wide with understanding. These were nuns you could marry! Julian hadn't lied. He'd brought him to something that was better than nuns. There was one problem...

"Julian, I get it. Sorry it took me so long and for my blunder with the ...well you know, but now I get it. I'm confused about a few things though. First of all, if he..." he gestured to Master Mucho who revealed his gold teeth again in a friendly smile, "...is so important, why does he want me to carry anything into Baboob?"

Julian shook his head sadly. “My friend, do you understand nothing? Haven't you been listening? The Babooban people are descended from Andorran smugglers. One of the great shames of their society is to pay taxes. That includes duties and tariffs. By smuggling contraband to Master Mucho's family you will be giving them great honor and, I might add, saving your own neck.”

Pig nodded his head. Contraband. Smuggling. What had he gotten himself into? Maybe he should go back to Vegas and get his old job back at the Hard Rock Casino. But then, as if on cue, another flock of Babooban girls streamed by wearing purples, pinks, blues, greens, reds, yellows and all manner of colorful silk habits that showed off their assets in the best possible way.

“Okay,” Pig said, “Is my name going to be a problem?”

To his surprise, Julian began to laugh. “Ha ha ha. Oh, that is funny. Ha ha ha.”

“I'm serious,” Pig whispered. “You said they don't like pig.” This was the first time he had ever referred to himself as Pig instead of Pigrone, which goes to show that one can become used to all things if given enough time and a semblance of normalcy. If you had asked him the year before if he would ever change his name to Pig, he would have told you that you were crazy. And, for the record, you might actually be crazy – I as the humble narrator have no way of judging your mental state — but back to Pig's dilemma.

Julian stood up, motioned for Pig to stand and wrapped a friendly arm around his shoulders as they looked out over the Babooban district. Flocks of Babooban girls moved from point to point. Young Babooban men were moving from shadow to shadow as if they were already the smugglers they dreamed of being.

“My friend,” Julian said in a warm conversational tone. “ I didn't say that the Babooban's don't like pigs. I said they don't eat them or sell them, so in that regard, you have nothing to worry about. Besides – before too long, I am sure that your name will be Mucho.”

As Julian reached into his pocket to pay Master Mucho of the Pickle Juice Tea the old man shook his head and pushed Julian's hands away.

“Bafia,” he said “Bafia.”

While he said the curious word, he motioned towards Pig and gave that gold toothed smile again. Then, with that same quickness, the old man was in front of Pig and kissing him on the lips. As he pulled away, he said “Bafia” again and Pig's face was washed in the smell of pickle breath.

“He won't let us pay,” Julian told him.”The word 'bafia' means family in Babooban. Master Mucho has become your Godfather.

Pig had come to Spain with some ideas that even he realized were dated by the time he was ready to leave. He'd pictured Spain as a kind of 'old Mexico' filled with fiestas and mariachi music.He was surprised that Spaniards didn't look like Mexicans or Columbians. Julian was as white as he was. He was disappointed to find that there were no authentic Spanish tacos or burritos and when he asked a waiter to bring him a quesadilla, he was shocked to be brought an omelet.

He'd read Ernest Hemingway's “For Whom the Bell Tolls” and so he was surprised to find that life in Spain didn't revolve around bullfights. In fact, Melody told the class that bull fighting would soon be made illegal! He'd thought that he would find women wearing Flamenco clothing and sipping sangria, but in fact, he hadn't seen anyone drinking sangria yet and when he asked Julian about it, the bartender laughed in his face.

“My friend, Señor Pig. Sangria is piss. It is the choice for the very poor made with the cheapest alcohol and the worst juice with the cheapest sugar added. My friend, sangria is for those who want to have a party but don't want to pay for everyone's drinks.” Pig was going to miss Julian. Who wouldn’t?

The two men had left the Babooban district and continued on an all night round of drinking through the ska, punk, and reggae bars until finally they stumbled home well after the sun had come up. Pig skipped the class on 'photocopies and lesson planning' in order to catch a few hours sleep

Teachers Learning Lessons

The last lessons of the TEFL class at ISHIT were about classroom management, discipline policy, and what to do when the school you took a job with decided to screw you and break your contract. It wasn't phrased exactly like that, but the instructors at ISHIT made it clear that at least half of the graduating teachers could expect to get reamed by a privately run language school

"Here's the breakdown," the female administrator explained to them using the whiteboard and a hot pink marker. She drew a circle on the board.

"This is your entire graduating class." She divided the circle into quarters. "This first quarter is for those who decide to go teach in Japan, Taiwan and South Korea." She shaded in half the space. "Those in the pink will have great jobs with high salaries and decent hours. Those in this other area that I am shading with hash marks will have one of those three things — great pay, a high salary, or a fantastic administration."

She grabbed a blue marker and dived the second quarter in two. "This is for those of you who are going to work in Eastern Europe, Indonesia, or South America. Half of you will have decent pay — not enough to live in the US or Western Europe but enough to live in Eastern Europe, Indonesia or South America. The schools will probably provide return airfare if you force them to honor their promise. They will also ask for long, but not intolerable hours and provide you with some holidays. The other half will have one of those things: time off, decent in-country pay, or housing." She marked the second half with blue hash marks.

The next quarter was a green marker. "Those of you who decide to work for either German companies, in Saudi Arabia or Bahrain, or who get picked up by NGO's can expect some benefits, decent pay, and housing to be provided. You will work long hours and be isolated from travel and leisure time, but you can expect to be well compensated. From looking at the class qualifications though — none of you have a Master's degree or a degree in English, so you can probably count on not getting these jobs." She divided a tiny portion of the circle. "One or two of you may get lucky. But the rest of you — if you work in these countries you can expect to get screwed somehow since you don't have the qualifications. So anyone that hires you is probably out to rip you off."

Finally she grabbed a red marker for the final quarter. "Those of you who have chosen to work in Africa, China, Turkey or anywhere else I haven't mentioned are heading into the wild-wild-west of TEFL. Regulation is light, exploitation is heavy, and perhaps one quarter of all the jobs in these places," she divided a small portion of the circle, "actually end up being pretty decent. But the other 95% ends up grinding through teachers without qualifications and using them until they quit or need to be fired."

"So," she turned to the class now. " To sum up – About 5% will get great jobs. Another 5% will get decent jobs. 1-2 % will get fantastic jobs and 3% will get lucky. The other 90% of you can expect to get screwed by some TEFL English mill. You probably should have taken more math classes and then you might end up with my job. Now...can anyone tell me what to do when you get the shaft from one of these companies?"

Melody, the dark haired girl raised her hand. The administrator motioned for her to speak. "We should notify the regulating body for TEFL and the Department of Education in the country we are working in. Then, we should post warnings to the various TEFL message boards and make sure the companies get black-listed from advertising with misleading job offers." Pig was impressed. She was pretty smart. She paused, "...but that's all I can think of."

The instructor nodded. "That's very good Miss. However, you forgot one thing." Melody looked pleased and waited expectantly. The rest of the class was writing down her suggestions except for Bob and Bing who were texting each other about the instructor's ass and how it looked in the grey tweed skirt she was wearing. She was a single mom, in her mid-30's, living in Spain as a way to get away from cold English winters where she couldn't wear short grey tweed skirts, and to escape her disgusting ex-husband. To be fair, her ass did look fantastic.

As the class looked on expectantly, Ms. Grey Tweed smiled at them and began. "The thing that you forgot is that there is no regulating body for TEFL, most of these schools aren't overseen by any department except the tax department, and if you report their behavior online they will add you to a 'no-hire' list and destroy your chances of ever teaching again. As for getting them blocked from the TEFL ad pages — those are paid ads so you won't be able to do it. Money wins in capitalism and you don't have any or you wouldn't be looking for these shitty jobs. So...the correct answer is... there's nothing you can do. You've decided to swim with sharks and since you aren't in the fortunate 15% if you are getting the shaft, you have to deal with it and see if you can get someone to write you a letter of recommendation and provide a good reference so that you can get another job. Any questions?"

The entire class sat there feeling stunned.

"Great." Ms. Grey Tweed began to erase the board. "Oh, wait. One more thing, you are much more likely to get a great job if you are attractive and flirtatious — even if you don't have the qualifications. Other than that, consider all of this a big adventure before you discover you would rather do something else with your life. Now, where do you all plan to go?"

She started with the younger members of the class who were mostly looking for jobs in Japan, South Korea, Taiwan, Europe, and then Melody who wanted to go to Peru. Next she asked Margot.

Margot turned to the class. "I want to say that this has been a pleasure, but I've been offered a job as an admin assistant with the Rick Steves Tours and so won't be teaching, but I wish you all the best of luck."

Bob and Bing followed up on Margot's surprise announcement with one that surprised no one. Both men had taken jobs in Pattaya, Thailand. They said their wages were about $7 a day, but they seemed happy to be in the location they had hoped for. They had already rented a house.

"And what about you, Sir?" Ms. Grey Tweed turned her attention to Pig now. Only Jenny and he had not answered.

Pig wasn't sure he wanted to tell anyone where he was going, but since everyone else had said, he felt obligated. “I'm going to go to Africa,” he said.

Ms. Grey Tweed wouldn't let him off the hook so easily. “Africa isn’t a country. Which country do you plan to go to? Morocco? Egypt? Mali? Niger? Sierra Leone? Africa is a big continent. Have you narrowed it down yet?”

“Actually, I have. I'm going to Baboob.” Pig spilled it out and was surprised to hear the rest of the class burst into laughter. He didn't understand exactly why they were laughing.

Ms. Grey Tweed understood perfectly. “Very funny Mr. uh...what is your name?”

“Pigrone,” he said. “Pigrone Martin.”

“All right then. Mr. Martin, what real country do you plan to go to? Are you actually going to Africa?”

Ms. Grey Tweed was giving him a very stern look as if she had caught him looking at her ass and texting his friend about it , which was what was going on elsewhere in the room.

Jenny came to his rescue. “Hey, fuck you bitch. It's a real country. I saw it on the fucking discovery channel. What kind of a horse-shit operation is this anyway? Is your geography as bad as your math?”

Apparently, Jenny was still off of her meds. Not only that, but she had an atlas in her bag which she pulled out and waved at Ms. Grey Tweed who came and took it with a knowing smile on her face as she flipped to the index and said “You see, there is no country called...oh wait...here it is. Sultanate of Baboob.” She turned to the North African page and looked at the tiny spots that are the Sultanate of Baboob. “Well, I'll be...uhm, wait, Miss...” she handed the atlas back to Jenny with apprehension. “Where are you going to be going?”

Jenny stood up and smiled at the class with her hair flowing out like blond static and a crazed look in her eyes. “I'm not going anywhere. I'm staying right here because I love mother-fucking Madrid. I got a job with ISHIT. I’m gonna be working with you.”

Pig was the only one that laughed.

The Secret History

Five days later, on the eve of his final exam for his TEFL certificate from ISHIT, Pig regretted not having asked Margot for her notes. What if there was a question about photocopies that he wasn't prepared for?

He had booked a flight to Rome. From Rome he would take a ferry to Tunisia. Once in Tunisia, he would take local transport to the border of Baboob. From there, he would need to hire a taxi to get him to the city of Turban, Baboob's capital. Making travel plans to Baboob was made harder by the fact that there was virtually no information about it on the internet and when he asked travel agents, they told him there was no such country.

He wanted to spend more time exploring Europe before heading to Baboob. It was not to be. Julian warned him that Master Mucho was expecting the repayment for the blood insult as soon as possible.

"What if I leave and forget about Baboob?" Pig asked, already beginning to wonder what it was he was going to have to smuggle into Baboob and worrying about the possible consequences. Maybe it was best to forget the curvaceous women of Baboob and their skin tight cloaks and colorful habits. Maybe he should stop imagining what it would be like to be a smuggler lord or to take part in the fascinating holidays Julian had been telling him about such as 'Graffiti Day'. It might be better...

Julian's hearty Spanish laughter from behind the bar of The Cock Bar, cut him off. "Ha, ha, ha. Oh, my friend, my friend. Please, do not even joke about that. I see that it is certainly a part of your American humor. Ha, ha, ha."

Julian's head came close to Pig's as he wiped the bar. In a low, strained voice he whispered "Do you have a death wish? The Baboobans hear all. Haven't you ever heard someone say, of a rumor that spreads like dandelion seeds, that it is on the 'Babooban wind.' Have you never heard 'the walls are the ears of Baboob'?"

Pig shook his head. "No, I never did."

Julian stood upright and began to polish glasses. "Besides, what man could ever forget the women of Baboob? For all of your life, you would dream of the Babooban feminine form and wish that you had honored the smuggle debt and found the woman of your dreams. You and I both know, my friend, that a man of high honor and principles such as yourself, could never leave a debt unpaid. It is unthinkable, no?"

Once again Pig was not sure whether to answer 'yes' meaning that it was unthinkable — even though he had left his student loan debt behind and not thought of it until this moment — or to answer no which would agree with the negative ending of Julian's sentence, but also seemed to contradict the sentiment of it being unthinkable. So, instead, he answered with the very neutral, and useful for such situations, "Of course."

He was pleased with the discovery that he could say something that affirmed and yet sounded so strong without actually saying anything. He had been reading as much as he could find about Baboob on the internet — which, to be honest, was not very much at all. So he threw in the famous adage "There is no war in Baboob."

Julian beamed brightly. "Indeed there is not! Oh yes, my friend, you have learned well. There is no war because the enemies of Baboobans either pay their debts or they die. Do you know, they say that the first Babooban Sultan was actually the famous Hasan i-Sabah, the Old Man of the Mountain?"

Pig had grown used to Julian's rapid changes of topic, but wasn't sure this counted as one at all.

"The who?" he asked.

"Hasan i-Sabah! Surely you know of Hassan? Do you know of Hassan and his assassins? Hashish? Have you heard of hashish?" Julian was looking worried, but Pig nodded brightly at the mention of hashish. He was from Vegas. There were very few drugs he wasn't familiar with.

Julian kept polishing the glasses as he explained.

“Hasan i-Sabah was a great scholar and scientist who discovered metaphysical secrets and great truths about the nature of reality in the tenth century. It is said, he used cunning alone to capture a great mountain kingdom between Persia and Syria. From his mountain stronghold, at Alamut, he would send his warriors to enforce his decrees throughout the Middle East. His soldiers were led to a religious ecstasy using an agricultural-chemical invention of Hasan i-Sabah — hashish. You see my friend, his name was Has-san and his product was Has-shish.”

“I never knew that,” Pig said. “I always thought it was because of corned beef hash – hey, did he invent that too?”

Julian nodded curtly, not really listening. “Of course he did.” He was eager to continue his narrative. “Hasan i-Sabah came to be called the ‘Old Man of the Mountains’ and was the virtual ruler of the entire Muslim world. He was the richest and most powerful person in all of history. Any time a ruler attempted to defy him, that ruler would be killed. A nice way to make people do what you want, no?”

“Of course,” Pig said, but for some reason felt like it didn't work as well this time.

“So, you can imagine, all the Muslim rulers were eager to have him out of the way. You can also imagine that for a scholar, scientist, philosopher and metaphysician, Hasan i-Sabah was spending way too much time sending out assassins — which word comes from 'hashishans' — by the way. He was far too busy with ruling the world to do what he really enjoyed. Not to mention every ruler for thousands of miles wanted to find a way to kill him.”

“But what does this have to do with Baboob?” Pig asked.

“It's simple. Hasan i-Sabah turned his mountain fortress over to his son and then faked his own death. He and his loyal followers came to a fruitful valley in Tunisia. There, he could focus on his religious, metaphysical, and scientific studies. It was there that he perfected Baoism, the religion of the Baboobans. They converted the local people and then along came Andorran refugees with a bunch of nuns and pirate families.”

“But I thought the chief of the Babooban's was humble? Didn't the Andorrans force him to become Sultan? And why is it called Baboob?”

Julian's laughter again filled the air. “Ah yes, Señor Pig. Certainly, he was humble but also he was perhaps the greatest player of the great game the world has ever seen. Hasan i-Sab-BAH...” he emphasized the last syllable “...controlled kings, sultans, and viziers. Many of them didn't even know he was the one making their decisions. In lands as far away as Italy, India, and the Central Asian steppes, it was Hasan i-Sabah who made leaders dance to his tunes. Do you think he wasn't able to manipulate the Andorrans? Do you think he wasn't able to bring them into his plans? By the way, did you know that in Hindi, Baboo means 'honored or respected person' and that in Persian it means father?”

“The Baboobans, of course, deny it. They claim to be descended from simple North African mountain nomads and Andoran traders, but if you ask me, I think Baboob has been in control of much more than the world realizes for as long as it has been around. The stronghold of the Hashishans was eventually wiped out in Syria, but Baboob has managed to sit unaffected for all of that time. It never pays to be too overtly political. I think that is the lesson Hasan i-Sabah learned.”

“Where do you learn all of this stuff?” Pig asked him.

“Bartenders know all the secrets of the world,” Julian replied.

Pig tried to digest it all, but mostly he was thinking (again) about how incredible the Babooban girls had looked. The way they dressed and moved, the way they looked at him...yes, of course he was going to Baboob.

“Of course I'm going to Baboob. Where will I pick up Master Mucho's package? What will I be carrying? Do you know?” Julian had been telling him to remain patient while he interfaced between Master Mucho of the Pickle Juice Tea and Pig. Every day, Pig asked and every day Julian told him to be patient.

“I'm afraid you will have to be patient my friend. Master Mucho has told me that you will be given the package in Rome before you board the ferry to Tunisia. The contents are a mystery. Sorry to keep you waiting.”

“Oh, it's not your fault,” Pig began before he noticed that Julian had moved down the bar to two women who had come in. His last words had been for them. It was six-minutes before he found his way back to Pig.

During that time, Pig thought of another question "How will they find me? I don't even know where I'm going to stay in Rome yet."

Julian looked intently at Pig. "My friend, the Baboobans can always find you. You may not see them until they want you to, but they are everywhere."

Failure

Pig studied for the ISHIT exam as if he were taking a final exam at the University of Nevada, Las Vegas. To be fair, UNLV isn't known for particularly difficult exams, but they still require a few days cramming if you haven't been paying attention in class. He set up a cram session which only Margot joined him at. He was surprised the others didn't care and surprised Margot did since she would be working for Rick Steves.

"Margot? I thought you weren't going to teach?" he asked her while they studied. She looked at him with a twinkle in her old blue eyes.

"I may not be teaching this year, but in sixty-five years, I've learned it's never a good idea to burn a bridge behind you. I've taken the course, so I'd like to earn the certificate... just in case." Pig didn't ask, but assumed the 'just in case' was in reference to her upcoming job not working out.

They studied late into the night with a particular focus on the photocopying session Pig had missed. When they walked into the classroom, Pig was as prepared as he had ever been. The instructor came into the class and handed out the exam, face down. He set a timer on his desk.

"You will have one hour to prepare a lesson plan for an intermediate class. You can teach them anything you like, but you must provide them with an entertaining hour which will help to improve their English skills. If you can't do this, you won't get your TEFL certificate."

He hit the timer.

Bob and Bing were done in ten minutes. They dropped their exams on the instructor's desk and went out to smoke. The younger members of the class were through in fifteen minutes. Melody took longer and was putting a lot of energy into her work. Jenny was using colored construction paper and a pair of scissors to cut out shapes. She had brought the paper and supplies in her giant handbag. Margot worked with her head down. They were the only three still working when Pig put the finishing touches on his lesson plan.

He would begin with an amusing fable. He chose the tortoise and the hare. After telling the story, he would ask the class what they thought it meant. Next, in the discussion period, he would ask them for different fables. Using handout photocopies made at the school prior to class, he would teach them about the past tenses, adverbs, and sentence construction. Finally, he would have the class write a fable of their own utilizing the lesson and finish with a small group session where they would read and discuss each other's fables. He was happy with it and realized that he really had learned how to teach English at ISHIT.

He placed his exam on the instructor's table and turned to walk out. Margot gave him an encouraging wink. Jenny was still cutting and pasting, and Melody was filling in a second sheet with small, tight script. He hoped he had done enough.

They were to return at 2:30 to learn their final grade in the course. Pig went to his dorm and slept until his alarm woke him. When he got back to the classroom, he found all the other students already there. The instructor looked annoyed. "Where have you been?" he demanded.

"I was sleeping. Am I late?" Pig was confused, which wasn't necessarily abnormal.

"No, but everyone else was early and we were impatient waiting for you." The instructor spoke with a lisp and had a bad comb-over across his shiny bald skull. "Very well. We can begin now."

The instructor looked through the stack of papers. First of all — "Who is Pigrone Martin?" Pig caught his breath. This couldn't be good. He raised his hand.

The man looked at him strangely. "Which of these exams is yours?" He held up Pig's and another which was certainly not his. His was the one on the right.

"Mine is that..." before he could point or say another word, Margot stood up, walked to the front of the class, and grabbed his paper.

"This one," she said firmly, "is mine."

"Hey, wait a minute, Margot, that's my...," she interrupted him.

"I'm sorry. We studied very late and I suppose I had him on my mind. I can't believe I wrote his name on my paper, but I'm old, you know and he reminds me a bit of my deceased husband. Let me fix this..." She scribbled out his name and wrote her own on his paper. "Pigrone, I apologize for my mistake." He wanted to correct her mistake, but the look she gave him forbade it. She handed the paper back to the instructor. "It was a silly mistake by an old woman. I'm sorry, Sir."

The instructor had lost his train of thought. "Um...Okay. Great. I have a few questions. First of all – Bob?"

Bob raised his hand.

"What movie will you show?" Pig could see that Bob had written only two or three sentences.

"I've always liked Midnight Cowboy," Bob said.

The instructor nodded. "Yes, a great film. And to make sure there was no cheating, Bing? Which movie will you show?"

Bing stood up. "I'd show a Steve McQueen movie. Maybe The Great Escape."

"Another fine choice. Congratulations. You are both teachers now. Grades are B for Bing and B for Bob" The two men stood and high-fived .

The instructor went through the rest of the exams. Most of the class had gotten A's or B's though there were a few C's. "Now, should we give the good news or the bad news first?"

He still hadn't given the scores for Margot, Jenny, Melody, or Pig. Pig was nervous, maybe he should have said something about Margot switching their exams. Why in the world had she done that? What was she trying to do?

The class roared "Bad news!" Since all of them had passed, they were happy to see someone else suffer.

"Very well," the instructor said. "The bad news is two of you failed the course completely and will need to retake it. First of all –

Margot. How can we possibly pass you when you state clearly that you will be making photo copies for students with the school's copy machine? We went over that — the students or the teachers have to pay, not the school. Fail."

Pig couldn't believe his ears. Margot failed? She was the best student, when they studied she'd known every answer, how in the world could she have...wait a minute. She'd switched her paper for his.

Margot stood up and took her paper. "It seems to me, the students are paying tuition and should get free handouts..."

"No handouts unless the teachers or the students pay for them. Is that clear?" Margot nodded and left the room with Pig's paper. As she walked out, she gave him a wink. She failed for him! It was the nicest thing anyone had ever done for him.

"Now, the second failure. You!" the instructor pointed at Melody. "These are the children of rich parents and you want to teach them about socialism, social justice, fair wages, unions, and equal rights? Totally inappropriate. Fail."

Melody looked stunned. As Pig stared at her, the instructor handed him Margot's paper which had his name written across the top. "Nice work. Second highest grade in the class Mr. Martin. However, the top honor goes to Jenny." He held up a huge poster of colorful animals with letters, punctuation, and stories written on it. "Creating a classroom activity that gets the students to talk about English using things they know. The kids will feel smart. They will feel like they are learning while they have fun. These students will go home happy and their parents will re-enroll them. Plus, you used all of your own materials and didn't cost the school a dime. Very nice work."

Pig was in shock. Margot had jumped on the grenade for him. If she hadn't, he would be sitting there mangled like poor bitchy Melody, who actually didn't seem like she was all that bad to him now. Maybe he had misjudged her. Now, she was left wondering what to do with her future just like he would have been if not for Margot. The big question was, why had Margot saved him? And how had she known he would fail?

The Bathroom Stall of Love

That night, Pig dreamed that the entire Babooban blood debt was a prank Julian was playing on him. When he woke, he couldn't convince himself it wasn't a prank. Julian had already known he was going to Baboob because, obviously, there was no other choice for a man with Pig's proclivities.

It was possible that the entire exchange between Master Mucho and Pig had been moderated by Julian, and for that matter, the whole thing might have been set up as a joke by his fun loving Spanish friend. That would explain why no one had brought him the package, given him any sort of communication, or anything else. The messages from Master Mucho went to Julian and then to Pig. It was an easy set-up. In fact, it made sense in a very mean kind of way, because he would wait for the package in Rome, never meet the Baboobans, worry about losing his life all the way to Tunisia, and then...

The idea of it all being some great hoax all fell apart as he pictured the gold toothed grin of Master Mucho of the Pickle Juice Tea. He remembered the way the cold steel of the knife had felt on his neck. He could still see the panic in Julian's eyes. If it was a hoax, he felt proud they had picked him as the victim of it. If it was a hoax, they were fine actors and he must be important enough to have gotten their attention. There was no way that was the case. It couldn't be a hoax.

Hoax or not, he was going to Baboob. He was also going to see some of Spain and Italy before he left. His last day in Spain, he strolled through the streets of Madrid, watched people on holiday, and admired the high style of young Spaniards.

They dressed smartly and stood with a casual electric energy as if they owned the streets. Their hair was done with meticulous precision into a couple of particular styles that Pig found himself wanting to mimic.They wore tight fitting jeans with bleached thighs and shins.

Legs tapered down to tight folds like the 'mods' had worn in the 80's when Pig was in high school. They wore designer t-shirts or brightly colored button-down shirts. For shoes — it seemed that shiny was in. Not only well buffed shoes, but shiny accessories on them as well. Big buckles, small mirrors in the laces, or super-glossy gloss-finished vinyl. These weren't dress shoes, they were sneakers that shined. All of that was trendy, but it was the jackets that Pig loved.

Young Spaniards wore stylized military jackets with lots of buttons, pockets, and tags but what set them apart was the big wolf-fur rimmed hoods. Pig thought of them as 'grunge-chic'. Actually, that was a fair term for a big portion of the Spaniard style.

Spanish style was all about highlighting the parts that mattered. For the women — ass, tits, legs, midriff, shoulders , no Spanish woman seemed willing to step outside without wearing something that pointed to the part she was most proud of. Round, abundant asses swelled in tight fitting jeans, short-short skirts over the top of tight wool stockings, and sweaters that may have been so difficult to pull over the boobs they engulfed that a lubricant was needed. Pig saw more nipple highlights on a short walk through Madrid than he would have in a seedy Vegas review. And their hair — the big hair of the 1980s held nothing on Spanish big hair. Gel, foam, spray, or sperm (because Pig had never been able to disassociate sperm with tight hold hair after seeing "*There's Something About Mary.*") Spanish chicks made hair into a three-dimensional art.

Pig never managed to get laid while he was in Madrid surrounded by these incredibly hot Spanish babes (not to mention the young, away from home and the USA for the first time, very, very easy American girls who were in his class at ISHIT)...you need to know that before he left for Spain, a few of his well traveled co-workers at the casino had given him some crude advice about chicks abroad.

"If it's pink, don't eat it. Always wear a condom with Euro chicks. Make sure she's not a tranny. See the vagina before you go too far. Be confident. Spanish chicks love macho men."

Pig wasn't sure the advice was good. His friends told him that Spain was rampant with transsexuals and venereal disease, but the girls he saw looked clean and they all definitely looked female. At least in his opinion — which didn't actually change the facts, only the way he looked at them. And besides, he thought to himself, 'They were probably tired of all the Spanish macho and wanted to meet a nice guy who would talk with them without feeling up their tits,' which was exactly what he wanted to do, but wasn't sure how to go about when he did meet Spanish girls — the feeling up the tits part, I mean.

Now, remember that Pig was a loser and you have to keep that in mind. He had no game. He was an incel before there was a term for it although sometimes he got lucky being in the right place at the right time with the right woman who didn't give a fuck ...or did. His best pick-up technique was to get so drunk he would forget he was self-conscious and then say something douchebaggy enough to women that they thought he was joking. Or maybe one of them would be drunk enough to start making out with him or agree to go back to his place or in some few cases her place, depending on whether she was leaving the next day or not.

So, the question remains, did Pig get to sample any delicious, yet dangerous Spanish sex? Did Pig get laid in Spain?

On his last night, he was drinking in The Cock Bar. Julian was behind the bar even though it had supposedly been his day off. The second bartender was ill, so he had to drag his hungover self from his apartment and come in to work. Pig sat at the bar working on crossword puzzles and sometimes picking up "For Whom the Bell Tolls" which he had bought earlier that day so he would have something to read on the plane. The Cock Bar was filling up as the evening progressed and Pig was becoming intoxicated.

"My friend," Julian warned him at midnight "Be careful, the night is still young but you already seem to be fading downward." He placed an espresso in front of Pig and refused to bring him another drink until he had drunk two more of the coffees.

It was while he was sipping the third espresso and looking at the Hemingway novel that Melody, the dark haired girl from class came in and sat beside him. She was obscenely drunk and looked at Pig with a cock-eyed look that was both confused and surprisingly friendly.

Pig had declined all of the invitations that had come his way that day — okay, really only two. One from Bob and Bing who were going to a club called "Sucia Sexy Sucia" or SSS. The other invitation was from Jenny who asked if he wanted to go to a midnight viewing of *The*

Rocky Horror Picture Show. He had always been creeped-out by *The Rocky Horror Picture Show* but never quite as much as imagining seeing it with Jenny next to him. Besides, he wanted to hang out with Julian – but then, he hadn't known Julian would be working. He had looked for Margot to thank her and ask her why she had saved him and how she had known, but the old woman had disappeared.

Melody giggled as she sat down and slurred a greeting of sorts at him. "You never really schtruck me as the type that reads....or does well on tests" she said as she crumbled onto a bar stool.

Pig turned to find a surprisingly friendly look from someone who had never seemed anything but hostile towards him. "Yes, I like books. Things are clean in books, I mean, I like that things get resolved. There is a start and a finish and everything that happens, happens for a reason." Pig was surprised to hear the words come out of his mouth. It must have been the combination of coffee and alcohol that had somehow loosened eloquence from his tongue.

"Yeah," she agreed. "Life is a real frucking mess." She giggled briefly."ISHIT, you shit, we all shit for bullshit. What a fucking joke, huh?" She nudged his arm to get him to chuckle with her.

"Hey," Pig said, "I think what happened today was bullshit. You really deserved to pass. I don't know why they would..."

"I'll tell you why," she spilled. "That ugly little fucker wanted a fucking blowjob that's why. It's always the same — dirty bald fuckers always have to pick on the smart hot girl. Well, he ain't getting it. I discriminate. You'd actually be pretty handsome if you were a little taller, a little more fit, maybe a little bit less you..."

Pig was more than a little surprised at her foul mouth, but far more surprised as she stood up and dragged him towards the bathroom "Come on," she whispered "you get the blowjob." And so he did. Pig had fucked in Vegas bar bathrooms before, but this was the first time there had been someone else fucking in the next booth.

As they were walking out towards the bar again, she gave him a sloppy drunk kiss and said "I've gotta go. I'm meeting my boyfriend at the dorms. Bye." As she walked out the door. Pig thought about asking her for her number but in a rare moment of clarity decided it didn't matter and she probably wouldn't give it to him anyway.

Pig asked for his bill and reached for his wallet. It was gone. Inside had been his Nevada drivers license, a condom (that had been there since 1997) and about four-hundred Euros. He'd left his credit cards, passport, and travelers checks back at the dorms. He couldn't help wondering if Melody had stolen his wallet. Spoiler alert, she had.

Julian brought the bill and Pig explained the problem. Julian shook his head “Oh, my friend Señor Pig, trouble seems to find you. You should go look in the bathroom to see if it dropped out while you were... resting.”

Pig found the wallet. It had been tossed into a urinal. He fished it out and found his driver’s license still there but the money and the old condom were both gone. Fun fact, stealing that condom changed Melody’s life and led to many wonderful things — but that is another story.

As for Pig, he was no Rick Steves. Rick Steves would never have lost four-hundred Euro getting a blowjob from someone who he didn't really know in a Madrid Bar... or would he? Pig thought it was possible as he considered it. Rick Steves was pretty cool.

Julian ripped up the bill and came from behind the bar to give Pig a giant hug. “My friend, Señor Pig, it is good to send you off smelling like sperm. Bring me something special from Baboob and never forget, the Baboobans are always watching.”

The next morning, Pig realized there should have been some sort of going away party or a time when the classmates could say goodbye, but if there was, no one told him about it. He looked around the studio dorms for someone to say goodbye to, but there was no one there. They had all been out drinking, he didn't want to go knocking on people's doors since it was 7 a.m.

The romantic in him considered leaving a poem for Melody with the dark hair, but when he grabbed a pen to write some a note, he was stumped by the fact that he didn't know what to say beyond the first stanza....

My money and my heart, now yours
In the bathroom stall of love

Tilting his Indiana Jones hat ever so slightly, he gave himself a roguish grin in the elevator mirror. This was the life of an adventurer.

Beautiful women, passionate love, and a lonely goodbye. Pigrone Martin, adven...

The elevator door opened on the ground floor and he was faced with the laughter of Bing and Bob. The two men were obviously smashed and coming in from a night out. Lipstick covered both of their collars and Bob's shirt tail was coming out of his open fly. Still, they were the ones laughing.

“Would you look at that giant pink suitcase?” Bob pointed at Pig's luggage.”Did you steal that from a whore, Pig? Did you put the whore in it? Bwah ha ha”

Bing wasn't going to let Bob have all the fun. “I've heard of backpackers before, but I've never seen a pack that so much needed to be taken back. My god... seriously what do you have in there? How much does that thing weigh?”

Pig tried to be good natured about their ribbing. “It was the biggest, cheapest bag I could find fellas. Hey, it's been nice knowing you.” Pig held out his hand. He had almost decided not to notify the authorities about them. Maybe their stories were just stories. It wasn’t his job to judge or condemn them. The truth is though, they were such assholes that he needed to do something with the journal full of atrocities he’d gathered about them.

“Hey, write the address of your new school down for me so I can send you some porn,” he said to them offering a manilla envelope that was just the right size to hold some smut mags — or the report he had compiled about them. It was an offer they couldn’t resist.

Bing pulled out a pack of cigarettes and put one in Pig's extended hand. “Have a fag you fag!” The two men laughed. Pig walked out of the building, into the Spanish post office, and sent the anonymous report to the school they were supposed to work at. He didn’t sign it or give a return address but he hoped that it would at least let someone know that they had hired predators who needed to be watched.

No one knows what happened to Bob and Bing. The last anyone heard of them they got on a plane to Thailand. The Thai authorities claimed they never entered the country. On one level what Pig had done was noble — on another it was cowardly. Still, he did the world a favor — of that, there can be no doubt.

Air O'Malley

He took the Metro to the airport where he checked into the budget airline on which he had booked his ticket to Rome.

"Welcome to Air O'Malley," the busty redhead at the counter took his passport and confirmation. "Do you have any checked baggage. Just one moment while I..." From the way she moved on, Pig guessed she was used to passengers with no bags to check.

"Excuse me," he said. "Yes, I do have a bag to check." Pig lugged his giant pink, hard case, security, wheelie bag up onto the scale. The digital numbers spun in circles but finally settled at ninety-five kilograms.

"I'm sorry sir, but our carry on policy limits your bag to five kilos and while we do allow a checked bag for an additional fee, the maximum weight is 32 kilos. I'm afraid I can't check you in until you resolve this. You can adjust your baggage over there" — she pointed to an area that Pig hadn't noticed.

People of all ages were frantically going through bags, sorting, rearranging, redistributing and repacking.

"How much is the extra baggage fee?" Pig asked.

The redhead cocked her head and smiled in a way that reminded him for some reason of a Golden Retriever. "Three hundred Euro but it also includes unlimited bathroom access and a free snack on your flight." Because of the very reasonable way she had said it, Pig actually nodded as if it were a good deal before he realized that it was more than three times the cost of his flight.

He moved over to the designated baggage rearrangement area, sat down and considered what was inside his bag. There were sixteen books he had brought with him. They were scholarly tomes about grammar, syntax, punctuation, and basic teaching principles. He also had seven novels he had already read and the new Hemingway novel which he had barely begun reading. He had seven pairs of shoes. Hiking boots, running shoes, walking shoes, wingtips, loafers, sneakers, and a pair of wool lined moccasins. He'd brought a camp stove (but had to discard the fuel bottle before leaving Vegas), a tent, a sleeping bag, a slingshot, a small cook-set, a rain parka, a heavy down jacket, four wool sweaters, three pairs of swim trunks, a Swiss army knife, twelve t-shirts, a suit, three ties, seven button down shirts, an alarm clock, an electric razor, a huge flashlight with four D-cell batteries, two rucksacks, a duffel bag, a travel chess set because he wanted to learn how to play, three bath towels, nine pairs of socks, six pairs of jeans, three pairs of trousers, three tubes of toothpaste, a toothbrush and an extra toothbrush in case he lost the first one, his laptop, power adaptors, and extension cords. There were also three ball caps, two wool hats, a pair of long underwear, four large chorizo sausages, a big block of cheese, half a pound of beef jerky he'd brought from home, and a box of Ritz crackers.

He sat for a moment thinking. "What would Hemingway do?" he wondered to himself. Pig figured Hemingway would throw it all away, swagger to the bar, get drunk, get in a fight, get arrested, miss his flight, and have some sort of adventure. Never mind what Hemingway would do. What would Pigrone Martin do?

He opened the bag and pulled out the smaller of the two rucksacks. He put his laptop, the new toothbrush, the rain parka, three pairs of underwear, three pairs of socks, a pair of jeans, a few t-shirts, one button down shirt, and a pair of swim trunks into the bag. Since there was still room, he added the sneakers he was wearing.

He decided to wear as much as he could so before putting the boots on, he pulled a pair of cotton trousers over his jeans, put on another pair of socks, another t-shirt, two button down shirts, and the down jacket.

"I'll leave the rest of this stuff here and someone else can take it," he thought looking down at the flashlight, alarm clock, books and other odds and ends. Putting *The Foreign Teachers Guide to Grammar and Classroom Management* in his right pocket and *Fun and Games for the TEFL Classroom* in his right pocket, he grabbed the Hemingway novel and put it in the inside pocket of the down jacket. Then he closed the bag and marched back up to the counter looking a lot more bulky than usual.

He put his rucksack on the scale. 5.6 kilos. He would have to get rid of something else. Or, maybe he could tip the scales. The redhead hadn't looked yet. He gave a touch of lift to the bag and it dropped to 4.8.

"Oh, I see you've adjusted things," she said. "Can I see your confirmation and passport please?"

They were in his security belt, under the jeans, under the cotton trousers. "Uh, just a moment..." Pig took his bag from the scale, unzipped his pants and opened the front buttons revealing his jeans. He undid the belt of his jeans, unbuttoned the fly, and unzipped the security belt. With all the extra layers, he was starting to sweat and his movement was restricted, but he managed to pull his passport and confirmation sheet out and put them on the counter. While he was in there, he pulled the security belt off and put it into the front pocket of the rucksack.

"Would you like a window or aisle seat?" the Redhead asked him.

"Window please."

"That will be thirty Euro for the window fee," she told him.

"Oh, the aisle will be fine.

"Twenty Euro for the aisle fee."

"Are there fee-less seats?" he asked.

"Are you willing to sit in the evacuation row?" she raised her eyebrows.

"Yes, that will be fine."

"Great, we'll need twenty Euro for the fresh oxygen and gate fee, plus another forty-five Euro for the restroom fee, and finally a thirty Euro fee for checking in." Pig had thought it was a discount flight.

After some haggling he managed to negotiate the additional fees down to sixty-five Euro which allowed him to use the bathroom twice, get checked in, and do a limited amount of breathing at no extra charge. He was the middle passenger in the evacuation row and would be required to participate in the safety demonstration.

The redhead handed him his boarding pass. "Thank you for flying with Air O'Malley. You can proceed through security and to Gate 72 using the courtesy van."

Pig moved over to the security line which must have contained a thousand people. As he watched the safety personnel, he was surprised to see many 'suspicious looking characters' waved through with no additional search but generally it was a certain type that was looked at with suspicion, asked to go to the search rooms, or who had their bags checked for bombs or drugs. He hadn't known that twenty-something blondes were such high-profile candidates for safety.

As he reached the x-ray machine a commotion broke out in the ticketing area. Looking back as he walked through the scanner, Pig was certain that the man who was supposed to be looking at the contents of his bag was actually looking at the ruckus behind him. Pig grabbed his bag from the conveyor belt and hurried towards the signs that said 'Air O'Malley Courtesy Van' but not before looking back to see what the disturbance was all about.

The baggage rearranging area was the center of the commotion. Three large German Shepherds stood around a giant pink suitcase and barked pleadingly while the handlers strained to hold them back on their leads. Everyone's attention was firmly fixed on the giant bag as another man scanned the bag with a hand held x-ray machine.

"Bomba!" he shouted and pandemonium began. Not pausing a second longer, Pig rushed in the direction of the courtesy van. He reached the waiting point and a brown 1970s Ford passenger van stood outside the terminal doors on the tarmac. Pig pushed the door open, stepped up to the van, and spoke to the driver.

"How long before we head towards Gate 72?" The van was dented and looked like something Bob and Bing would be hiding in except for the huge "Air O'Malley Courtesy Van" logo on the side of it.

The blonde English kid looked at him with a big smile. "We have to wait until someone pays the twenty Euro Courtesy Van fee."

"Great, let's go." Pig handed the blonde kid a twenty Euro note.

The van left the airport, got onto a small country road and drove for fifteen minutes before arriving at a small landing strip in a big agricultural field. A medium-sized jet dwarfed the small, very new terminal building which had a big red 'Gate 72' written on it.

Walking into the building Pig was met by the same Redhead from the ticket counter: which seemed to defy some sort of physical law, but he decided not to think about it.

"Welcome to Air O'Malley. Flight 1139427 to Campiano, Rome is now boarding. Please proceed to the boarding ladder. May I see your boarding pass please?"

Pig handed her the boarding pass and gave her a smile but there seemed to be no recognition as she smiled back at him.

"Thank you, would you like to beat the rush and pay a thirty Euro priority boarding fee?" Pig declined and was led to the aircraft straight away. He was surprised there was no ramp, but the ladder worked perfectly well. There was a scissor jack nearby, presumably for the handicapped passengers.

On board, he was met by the same blond youth who had driven the courtesy van, but the boy offered only the same big, white-toothed grin. "Welcome to Air O'Malley, would you like to upgrade to Middle Class for a twenty Euro fee?" Again, Pig declined and he was led to his seat in the emergency exit row.

Pig wanted to ask what had happened back at the main terminal with his pink bag, but didn't want to make anyone suspicious of the fact that it was his giant, pink, meat filled bag that seemed to be causing all of the problems.

"Ladies and Gentlemen, Welcome to Air O'Malley. If you'd like to purchase a head rest, pillow, or to have us remove the legroom blocks under the seats in front of you there will be a thirty Euro fee. Now, we'd like you to pay attention to the safety briefing and buy lottery tickets from our flight crew."

"You're up," the blond kid motioned to Pig. Pig had no idea what to do. He stood up and moved to where the blond kid was.

"Go on," the kid nudged him. "What are you waiting for? Give them the safety briefing!" Pig had only flown from Vegas to New York and from New York to Madrid but he figured he could do it.

"All right," he said. "First of all, fasten your seat-belts like this." He sat and put on a seat-belt, then took it off and stood up again. "No need to make them tight. In the event of a crash..." the blond kid elbowed him in the ribs and whispered "Emergency".

Pig continued. "In the event of an emergency. Put on the air mask." The blonde kid interrupted him now.

"But only if you have paid the additional oxygen fee of thirty Euro."

Pig went on. "And then, proceed to this row where I am sitting and I will help you out the emergency exit."

The blonde kid motioned him back to his seat. "Good job." And now it was the Air O'Malley staff who took over. "In the event that you would like help from our professional staff you can purchase the emergency upgrade for one-hundred Euro. If you purchase the emergency upgrade you will be assisted by our professional flight crew and allowed to exit the first class emergency exit door. You will be allowed to exit the aircraft before all the other passengers..."

An announcement came over the intercom and interrupted his spiel. "Flight crew prepare for takeoff. We have been moved forward in our departure time because of the bomb threat at the main terminal."

The flight crew scrambled to their seats and strapped themselves in while passengers called out that they would like the emergency upgrade. Apparently bomb scares were good for business. Either that or Pig had been less than inspiring in his safety briefing. Actually, it was both.

The Evacuation Row

The seats on either side of Pig were a study in contrasts because of the character, shapes, and colors of the inhabitants. On the thirty-Euro-window-fee side there was the whitest woman Pig had ever seen. Her skin was whiter than snow. It was blinding. An alabaster complexion of such downy brightness that one would almost think she was a statue come to life. This incredibly white woman, however, wasn't white at all.

To Pig, that was the surprising thing: that a non-white person could actually be more white than a white person. It made him feel positively pink and red to be next to her. She was a tiny Japanese woman about twenty-eight-years old. She wore brightly colored trekking gear made of state of the art synthetic material designed to breathe, allow moisture to escape, protect from all weather, UV radiation, and make the person wearing it visible for many miles because of the reflective quality of the bright colored synthetic threads. She didn't really need it — not for visibility.

Pig was looking out her window when she turned to him with a smile. He smiled back, marveling at the brightness of her clothing, her skin, and her teeth.

"*Konnichi wa*," she said and being a man of the world, Pig knew that it meant hello, but not what language it was.

"Hello," he said back to her. "Are you Korean?"

She shook her head no. Pig wondered if he should guess again. His mother once told him that Asians hate it when you try to guess their nationality or ethnicity, but she was still smiling at him so he felt obligated to say something.

"You look Chinese or maybe Thainese," he pointed "Go to Rome?" He made the motion of an airplane with his hand — at least he thought that was what he was doing but .really he was just rocking his hand back and forth.

She shook her head no. He wasn't sure to what so he made bird flapping motions with his arms. "Go ROME?" he said it louder because that always helps.

"Hi!" she said to him brightly.

"Oh, hello," Pig said, slightly confused because he thought they had already done this part.

"You," he again pointed at her "Fly. Rome?" This time he put his arms out like a bird, made jet noises, and then drew a halo on his head, thinking of Caesar and his crown of leaves. She was sure he was a mental patient at this point.

"Hi!" she said to him, nodding but frowning because she thought they had already had this part of the conversation and she had answered him.

"Yes, hello," Pig thought maybe it was the only word she knew in English. He decided to try a different question.

"Me." he thumped himself on the chest "Pigrone. You." Now he pointed at her. No response. "Do you understand?"

"Hi!" she said to him with a big smile. Before he could say hello again she continued. "You," she thumped him on the chest. "Pigu! Hi!"

He frowned because it seemed like no matter how hard he tried, no one would call him the name he wanted to be called. Still, perhaps she was a little bit off her noggin. Would anyone who was sane wear such bright colors? "You," he pointed and then raised his hands up in the universal sign of a question with palms to the sky and shoulders shrugged, elbows bent.

"Hi!" Pig decided to give up, but his new friend wanted to show that she understood. "You-" she thumped his chest again "Pigu." Now she thumped her own chest "Me. Hi!"

"Okay, whatever." She, however, wouldn't give up. "You-" she took his hand and thumped his chest with it "Pigu" Now she put his hand on her chest. "Me. Hi."

Pig still didn't understand so she took his hand and brought it to her small bosom again, this time rubbing it over them. "Hi. Hi. Hi. You stupid Pigu. Namae wa Hi. Me. Hi. Hi. Hi. Hiiiiiiiii." Pig felt the tiny nipples suddenly jutting out of the lycra jumper she wore as she rubbed his hand across her breasts again. “Hi.”

“Hi!” he said, mostly to himself. It caused the woman to squeal with delight; so much so that he thought perhaps he had figured it out. He decided to see if he was right.

“Me,” he said trying to ignore the stiffening of his cock as she still rubbed his hand on her chest. “Stupid Pigu.” He found himself using the name she had given him, after all, it's hard to be annoyed with a woman who is forcing you to feel her boobs. ”You-” he emphasized the word for effect “Hi.” It seemed appropriate to him to give her little titty a squeeze as he said her name.

She nodded a friendly but curt nod “Hi.”

He decided to confirm it by giving the other titty a squeeze. “Hi?”

This time he was met with a tiny alabaster hand slapping his face. “You dirty Pigu!” With that, Hi turned towards the window to watch the Mediterranean coastline and gave him the view of her angry stone shoulders. The slap hadn't made the erection go away.

“She's Japanese,” the man on his right side (in the twenty-Euro-aisle-fee seat), said to him. “Her name is Hi but hai, which is pronounced hi, is also the Japanese word for yes. It's confusing, as you've no doubt noticed. I'm Kai.”

Kai held out his giant black hand. As white as Hi was, Kai was blacker. As petite as Hi was, Kai was gargantuaner (if there was such a word). He wasn't muscular, he was fat. Kai filled his seat and spilled into Pig's seat, spilled into the aisle, spilled into every available space in the compact row. Pig wondered why it was only he that had to give the safety briefing but realized that Hi spoke no English and for Kai, the act of getting up would be a mammoth (ha ha) undertaking. It was only because they were in the emergency row that Pig had been able to get by him at all.

“Hi Kai. I'm Pigu-” he paused for a second “-rone. Pigrone.”

Kai's voice was gentle and for a man of his size, astoundingly high-pitched. “Pig-a-roni – the San Francisco Treat!” Kai sang the TV jingle in one of the sweetest voices Pig had ever heard. Then he stopped suddenly and said in a conversational voice “Grab my breast.”

Pig didn't really know what to say, but what was left of his erection was instantly gone. “What?”

"Hi is watching. You offended her by squeezing her breast like that. If you squeeze my man-boob, she will think it's something that you do to everyone. Just do it." Kai's logic seemed sound so Pig reached out and gave the man's gigantic man-mammary a squeeze.

"Nice to meet you Kai," Pig said, squeezing the man-jug a couple of times for good measure. At that moment, the flight attendant came by.

"That's enough," Kai said.

"Sir," the blond kid asked Kai. "Is this man bothering you? Because if he is, you might want to consider purchasing the O'Malley Air anti-harassment package for 10 Euro. It includes..."

"No thank you, Bra." Kai said. "No problems." Kai reached down and removed Pig's hand from his man-bosom. When the flight attendant arrived, Pig had simply frozen with his hand there. He turned toward the window only to have a pair of tiny white hands shoot out and grab his own boobs "Hi," Hi said. Kai had been correct. Big brains in the big body.

Over the course of the flight, the cabin crew attempted to sell snacks, maps, calendars, lottery tickets, hotel discount coupons, girl scout cookies, barf bags, crystal radios, and souvenirs from both Madrid and Rome as well as Irish souvenirs for good measure. They offered tiny bottles of booze, duty free shopping, and bus tickets to take the passengers from the distant Campiano Airport to the center of Rome.

"How much are the bus tickets?" Pig asked the blonde kid.

"Twenty Euro," was the answer. Kai looked at Pig and shook his head no. When the blonde kid was gone the big man explained.

"The cost of transport is directly proportional to how far you get from the arrival gate. If you buy the ticket now the cost is twenty Euro. Once we get there, you will see vendors at arrival selling for fifteen Euro. When you go through baggage claim it drops to ten Euro. Once you step through customs they sell them for six Euro and if you go outside directly to the Eurovision bus, it will only be four Euro. It's almost always best to wait. Where you are staying in Rome?"

It was something that Pig should have planned, but hadn't. He didn't have an answer so he decided to lie about it. "I like to stay at Caesar's when I'm in Rome," he said.

Kai looked at him suspiciously “Caesar's?”

Pig nodded. “Yes, Caesar's Palace.”

Kai looked serious and then laughed. “Bra, you from da ninth island aren't you?”

Pig didn't know what he was talking about.

“Vegas, Bra. The ninth island of Hawaii. You're from Vegas, right?”

Pig suddenly understood. Hawaiian's called Vegas the ninth island of Hawaii because there were more Hawaiians there than any place other than Hawaii. He’d heard it before, but like most things he heard in Vegas, he’d forgotten it. Las Vegas was the number one vacation destination for Hawaiians and they all seemed to stay at the California Hotel while they were there. Many of them had moved, thus creating the ‘ninth island'.

“You're Hawaiian?” Pig asked.

“Yeah, Bra. Kai stands for Kailanianiole Mokapu Kaneshiro Mehele Kapaapononahuihui. You got no place to stay in Rome?”

Pig reluctantly admitted it. “I figured a huge city like Rome would have plenty of places to stay.Was that a mistake?”

Kai shook his head. “Rome is filled with hotels and they are constantly full. And Bra, so you know- there ain't no Caesar's Palace in Rome. Also, no Stardust, no Sahara, no Circus Circus, but there is a Waldorf Astoria — that’s where I’m staying.”

Hi had been listening to the conversation. Suddenly she started saying something in a very excited voice that definitely included Kailanianiole Mokapu Kaneshiro Mehele Kapaapononahuihui – all in very fast Japanese.

Kai responded in the same language and the tiny white Japanese woman and the humungous black Hawaiian had a conversation in Japanese over Pig as if he weren't there for the next ten minutes.

The flight crew announced that passengers should return to their seats but could purchase an additional 'safe landing cushion' for five Euro. Kai and Hi finished up their conversation. Hi looked at Pig while Kai explained.

“I'd love to offer you a place to stay, but I'm meeting my mom and aunties at the Waldorf Astoria and we're going to be sharing a suite there. It sounds like you might be in luck though. Hi is staying at a hostel near the center and she said you should come with her and they will probably have space. That's probably your best bet. If you guys get the chance, I'll add you to the guest list and you can come see my show at the Waldorf Astoria tomorrow night."

"Your show?" Pig had wondered why Hi was so excited when she heard his name. Now he understood. Kai was famous.

"Yeah," Kai said. "I play the ukulele. Look, when you get off the plane, go with Hi."

Pig turned to Hi and said "Okay?"

Her little white hand shot out and gave his titty a squeeze as she said "Hi!"

After the plane came to a stop, Kal stood up and effectively blocked anyone from passing by the aisle thus allowing Pig and Hi to grab their carry-on bags and be among the first off the plane. As they started down the exit ladder, Kal called to them"Don't forget, you're on the list for my show at the Waldorf Astoria tomorrow night. It's a dinner show so don't eat before you come!"

He repeated the same message to Hi in Japanese and she waved and said "*Sayonara*!"

On the ground she grabbed Pig's hand as if he belonged to her and rushed him towards the terminal while with her other hand, holding her bag over her head to protect her from the sun: which was already fairly well hidden behind a cloud, the terminal building, and was almost below the horizon.

Pig's travel expectations were again met with a completely different reality as he waited to get his passport stamped at customs and didn't get a stamp at all.

"Aren't you going to stamp it?" Pig asked the Italian immigration officer.

"No!" The man said it so firmly that Pig was too intimidated to ask again. The man's steel blue eyes stared at him as if daring him to say something. Pig didn't dare. He took his unstamped passport and walked towards customs where he expected the smartly dressed customs officials to search his bag and ask him about what he was carrying. Hi caught up with him and grabbed his hand again.

The customs officers didn't even look at them as they walked through the doors marked "Nothing to Declare". Pig wondered if it would always be so easy to enter another country but then realized Europe was really like the United States now, so he had only gone from one state to another.

No Room to Rome

Pig was excited to see Italy and Rome. In truth, dear reader, one should remember, that in a sense, it was the herpified drunk Italian woman who really started this whole adventure. Also, keep in mind that while Pigrone wasn't his given name, perhaps part of the reason he liked it was because it sounded so incredibly Italian. Finally, when it came down to it, Venice and Caesar's Palace, in Pig's opinion, were the two best casinos in Vegas. So, you might have an idea of how excited Pigrone really was as the Air O'Malley flight brought him into the most famous city in the world.

As Kal had said it would, the price for the bus got lower and lower as Hi led him to the Eurovision bus across the lot. Pig stopped to have a smoke and Hi looked at him impatiently and said some things in Japanese that Pig figured meant that smoking was bad for him. He knew. Did anyone who told a smoker about how bad it was for them ever think they were the first or that the smoker didn't already know?

The Eurovision bus was four Euro which made it one of the great values of Europe as far as Pig was concerned. Not a single thing on Air O'Malley was less than five Euro and here was a big luxury bus for four Euro. Awesome.

"Termini?" the driver said as Hi dragged Pig by the hand to the bus and indicated that he should pay.

"Hi." Hi said.

"Oh, Hi!" the driver said back to her "Are you going to Termini?"

"This happens a lot" Pig said. "Yes, Termini is the center?"

"Si," the driver said as Hi said "Hi" and gave her four Euro fair to Pig who had thought she was going to make him pay for her.

The confusion with her name really did happen frequently. Everywhere she went, Hi was certain that people were talking about her since she always heard her name spoken by strangers. She thought she was quite famous, but in truth, she was a very white Japanese girl with a funny name and a cute smile and a bit of madness.

On the bus, Hi pulled a sheaf of papers from her bag and showed them to Pig. He couldn't read them since they were in Japanese, but the map of Rome she handed him was written in English and Italian.

She pointed to the airport which was clearly marked and then followed the road with her finger to a big area called Termini. She looked at Pig meaningfully and said what he thought was "Do you understand?" but really was "What are you doing here?"

Pig nodded in the affirmative. Realizing she would get no answer, Hi began to look for where her hostel was located on the map. Her papers said it was near Termini but she didn't understand English or Italian so she had hoped the man next to her (Pig) would be able to help, but he seemed either unwilling or unable, though she thought him very confident with his knowing smile.

Pig felt as confused as he ever had in his life. How in the world had he ended up in Rome with a cute Japanese woman he had no language in common with looking for a hotel? Was the incredible sexual fantasy he was beginning to hope he was living actually going to happen? He had no idea. He could only smile stupidly while she attempted to explain whatever it was he didn't understand: which was everything she said. I will give you another spoiler and tell you that no, Hi had no sexual interest in Pig and his imagination was the only place where there was even the remotest possibility of that happening.

As has been mentioned before, this is not a travelogue, so I will pass on mentioning the stunning views of the Parthenon, the Coliseum, or how Pig felt that all of this was eerily familiar; but couldn't recognize that his having seen La Dolce Vita had made that feeling inevitable. Never mind that the stunning contrasts of the huge and pompous palaces and classic architectures side by side with the tiny old houses and shabby concrete buildings made him giddy with excitement. Forget that for at least a few minutes he was able to forget about his fixation with nuns, Baboobans, and tiny white Japanese boobs, while he looked out the window at cramped cobbled streets and wide basilica-lined avenues, because after all, this isn't a travelogue.

The bus took an hour to get to Termini. Fifteen minutes of waiting for the bus to fill and then forty-five minutes of driving. When it stopped, there was no bus terminal in sight. It halted on a road lined with dirty shacks made of cardboard and bed-sheets. The villas of the Roman homeless. Shanties lined the wall of a very large shopping mall. Assuming Hi knew what she was doing, Pig followed her off the bus and only then realized she didn't know at all.

She looked around for someone who looked like they spoke Japanese, but the only person who might have was a very filthy Asian bum with a giant sack of cans on his back. He wore a camouflage coat that probably hadn't been washed in three years. Underneath the dirt and grime, he looked like he might be Japanese.

Hi called out to the bum in Japanese. “Konnichiwa.” He turned and looked at her, dropped his cans, and ran faster than Pig would have thought possible. It was starting to get dark and as the bum ran away, Hi grabbed Pig's hand and they attempted to give chase. The bum was faster than he looked and lost them after two and a half blocks. In the winding streets around Termini, it was far enough for Pig and Hi to be totally lost.

The sun was down and the two of them walked the streets, neither one sure of what the other was looking for. Finally, Hi found her goal: and it's not surprising that Pig didn't find what he was looking for since he was only following Hi. What she found was a Sushi bar.

As she dragged Pig in, he realized he was hungry, but he wanted his first meal in Italy to be pizza. He hesitated but she was insistent. Inside, she pulled out her papers and rushed to the Sushi bar. The Sushi chef answered all of her questions, gave her directions, pointed out where to go, and seemed to be very helpful. He also asked what she was doing with the strange white guy.

“He's mentally ill,” Hi told sushi-man, which was what she had come to believe. “I'm helping him find a place to stay.”

The two talked for ten minutes. Pig wasn't sure if he were asking her if she understood or what her name was, because either way, her answer to almost everything he said was “Hi”. Ultimately it didn't matter.

Pig had resigned himself to eating sushi in Rome. In fact, he had decided it would be one of those quirky experiences that travelers love to share, but Hi grabbed him and pulled him out of the restaurant without so much as a spicy ahi roll. Having gotten her directions straight she led him right to the Central Rome Hostel.

Up four flights of stairs, through three security doors, finally they were at the reception desk. As they were going up the stairs, two heavily laden Indian guys were heading down the stairs with disappointed looks on their faces as they lugged their many shopping bags and huge suitcases.

The man at reception spoke excellent Japanese. He also spoke English and fourteen other languages. He was vastly underemployed. Hi had reserved a dorm bed in the women's dorm. Once she was through checking in, Pig asked if they had any vacancies in the men's dorm.

"No," the clerk replied. The same answer he had given the two Hindus earlier. The answer was no. Pig asked if they had any private rooms. The answer was no. Pig asked if the desk clerk could recommend anyplace else.

"If you hurry," the desk clerk told him "You should be able to catch those two Indians I just sent to one of our sister properties. They've got a three bed private and you are unlikely to find anything else in Rome since there are four big conventions happening here over the next three days."

It had been five minutes since they'd passed the Hindu's. If he were going to catch them, he needed to run.

"Go out the door, go right, go three blocks and they know the rest of the way. You should be able to catch them if you hurry. I don't think they'll move very fast with all their luggage."

Pig turned to Hi, his fantasies involving her dashed to the ground. "Bye, Hi." He rushed out the door hearing a rush of Japanese from Hi to the desk agent.

As he reached the stairs, the desk agent called out "She says to come meet her for breakfast at 9 a.m. tomorrow! It's on us. Good luck." Pig smiled. Maybe there was hope. Right now though, he needed to find the Hindus and convince them to let him share their room.

He ran down the street, glad he had abandoned his possessions in the Madrid Airport. Ahead, he saw two figures trudging along under too much stuff. It was dark so he yelled “Hey, Indian guys, wait up.” They either didn't understand or weren't listening.

“Hey...” he was close enough now that they must have heard him. He kept running, hearing his feet echo off the sidewalk and onto the surrounding buildings. “Hey...wait.”

Just as he caught up, the Indians dropped all of their bags and ran in opposite directions from him. Pig stopped, surrounded by their possessions but not sure whether to look left or right since they had abandoned each other and their bags, whether by design or by purpose.

“Hey,” Pig yelled out. “Wait! Don't run. I'm from the hostel. The hostel guy told me to catch up with you and see if you would let me take the third bed. Really, wait, I don't want your stuff...Hey, come back.”

Pig looked to the right and saw one man come out from a bench he'd hidden behind. To the left, the other man emerged from an alleyway he had bolted down.

“Oh, you're from the hostel, are you? How can we know you aren't lying and waiting to kill us?” the first Indian said.

“Manev. He is telling the truth. I saw him on the stairs...he is from the hostel,” the second man said.

“You want to pay for one third of our room? This is acceptable to me. Abhay, is this acceptable to you?” he asked Abhay.

“No Manav. He is taking space from us so I think he should pay more than each of us. We pay half and he pays the other half. Certainly this is acceptable. So it is decided. Let us go then.” Abhay and Manav picked up their bags and packages.

They didn’t give him a chance to negotiate and actually, he didn’t have a choice.

“Thank you. I'm Pigrone.”

“I am Manav and my colorful friend with the many packages is Abhay. It is very nice to share the road with you Pig-man.”

“And thank you for not robbing and killing us,” Abhay added.

Pizza Nuts

They checked into the hotel and went to their shared triple room. Pig thought about how unprepared he had been for Rome. For that matter, he had been unprepared for Spain, he was unprepared for Tunisia, and certainly he hadn't done anything to prepare for his journey to Baboob.

As Manav and Abhay thumbed through their copies of *The Rough Guide to Rome*, *Lonely Planet's Rome,* and *Rick Steves Guide to Rome*, Pig tried to figure out why he seemed to be the only person on the planet who didn't have a guide book or reservations for his next leg of travel. It wasn't that he was adventurous. It was that he was clueless.

It wasn't a part of a grand plan or a moral objection to planning or guide books. Instead it was something he hadn't thought of until now. He'd thought of enrolling in the course, he'd thought of buying the plane ticket, but that was it. In Vegas, people didn't make plans. Instead, you simply went until you found the best deal. Usually, you didn't have to leave the strip to find a $5.99 steak or a hotel room for $30.

'Besides,' Pig thought, 'if he'd of made plans he wouldn't have had the crazy adventure with Hi or be sharing a room with his new friends Manav and Abhay.'

He wouldn't have been able to go to The Sultanate of Baboob, because he would have already made plans. Somewhere along the road of his life, Pig had heard the phrase 'Life is what happens when you are busy making plans' and he'd internalized that as 'Don't bother making plans' or 'Plans fall apart – so don't make them."

Still, he did have a plan. It just wasn't a plan he had made, instead it had sort of fallen on him. A very loose plan. He was going to spend the next day exploring Rome and then he'd catch the ferry to

Tunisia. It wasn't much of a plan at all. He didn't even know if there was a ferry to Tunisia, but he figured that since the original Babooban nuns came from Italy, it was probably a place where you could find a way to get to Baboob. It was a terrible plan.

He was hungry. He was in Italy. He wanted Pizza.

“Hey guys. You want to go get some pizza?” The Indians looked at each other and then said in unison. “Yes.”

Grabbing their guidebooks and leaving their bags behind, the three left the hostel and went in search of a pizza joint. Since they were in Rome, it didn't take them long to find one. There were pizza joints on every street, sometimes five in a row and all next door to each other. The hard part was deciding which pizza joint to go to.

Ultimately, the decision was made for them when a skinny dark skinned man in a giant white pizza chef hat – called out to them in English “Hey, Hindus and white boy — come eat here. We've got the best pizza in Rome.”

The Indians ignored the man until he started speaking Hindi. The Hindi decided them. Inside were a dozen pizzas under the glass counter.

“How much is this one?” Pig asked.

“It depends on how much it weighs,” the pizza chef answered.

“And this one,” Pig now pointed to a calzone.

“It depends on how much it weighs,” the pizza chef answered. And then he screamed “WHOOOOOP AAAHA”

Manav jumped out the door of the shop, Abhay scooted back against the wall, and Pig nearly jumped out of his skin. The pizza chef stood there looking at them all as if he hadn't just shouted a crazy sound and scared the hell out of them.

“It all depends on the weight. It's fourteen Euro per kilo.” The pizza chef wasn't even smiling.

Manav had come back into the shop.

“You guys want to share a pizza? We can get him to make us a fresh one.” Pig suggested.

“No,” Abhay said. “We're vegetarians. You won't want to eat with us.”

“Sure, I do. I don't mind eating with vegetarians,” Pig said, confused as to why they would think he was prejudiced against them.

"No," Manav explained "He means you won't want to eat pizza with us because we don't eat meat. You won't want the same kind of pizza we want. You should order something for yourself."

"Okay," Pig said. "Do you have any pizza with nuts on it?" Pig liked cashews on his pizza.

The chef pointed to a thick cheesy pie with artichoke hearts, tomato, and pesto. "This one has pine nuts in the pesto."

"Okay," Pig said.

"WHOOOOOP AAAHA," the pizza chef again scared the hell out of the three of them again with his sudden outburst. The other people in the shop looked as if they hadn't even heard him. He picked up Pig's slice and put it in the oven to warm. He turned to the Hindus.

"What about you guys? Want to try some beef?" the pizza chef was grinning now. Huge white teeth. Manav and Abhay were not smiling. "Come on, a joke. Can't a Bangladeshi kid mess around with a couple of Indians?"

The two Indians turned away and went five feet from the counter where they had a whispered conference in Hindi. They came back a moment later. "We'd like you to make us a cheese pizza with pepperoni."

Now it was the Bangladeshi's turn to lose his grin. "Hey, come on. I was kidding. I can make you a vegetarian friendly pizza."

Abhay stepped closer to the counter. "We're not in India anymore and no one is watching us. I've always wanted to try pepperoni and I don't mind that it's pig or even cow. Cow's aren't sacred in Italy, are they?"

Pig found himself annoyed. "I thought you guys didn't want to share a pizza because you were vegetarians? I wouldn't have minded getting a pepperoni pizza."

"WHOOOOOP AHAAA," the chef was standing there looking like he hadn't just shrieked like a monkey — again. "Okay, one pepperoni coming up."

"We are vegetarians," Manav said. "But the truth is, we didn't want to eat from the same pizza as you. It's hard to explain. We didn't want to offend you."

"But you ordered a pepperoni pizza? How can you say you're vegetarians?" Pig was trying hard not to be offended.

“Most Hindus that come to Rome do far worse than that while they are here,” the Bangladeshi pizza chef said from under his puffy pizza maker's hat.

“Like what?” Abhay asked.

“WHOOOOOP AAAHA! Rome is a city filled with whores, bars, and gambling. What do you think they do? Nobody comes to Rome for the beaches.” Pig hadn't even jumped that time when the man had shrieked. Beaches reminded him of his need for a ferry.

“Hey, do you know if there is a ferry from Rome to Tunisia?”

The pizza chef shook his head. “Nope. You're going to have to take the train to Civitavecchia and catch the ferry from there. It takes two hours.”

“Just two hours to get to Tunis?” Pig said.

The Bangladeshi laughed. “Man, you're an idiot. Two hours to get to Civitavecchia .Where'd you find this guy?” He asked the two Hindus.

“He chased us down the street,” Manav said.

“We don't really know him,” Abhay said. “He's not our friend. We don’t even like him but he paid for half our room.”

“WHOOOOOP AAAHA!” the Pizza Chef shrieked.

Pig was speechless. Were all Indians and Bangladeshis this rude and crazy?

The Freaks

Back at the hostel, the clerk asked where they had eaten. When they told him, he laughed. “Haha, Chef Whoopa. He’s famous. He’s not Italian but he’s studied with some of the greatest pizza makers in the world. I like his pizza, but I think his turrets might actually be a part of his success. In Rome, we love characters.”

Pig had a hard time sleeping. The Hindu's had been friendly with him and he had thought they had become friends until the bizarre incident in the Chef Whoopa’s pizza shop. The two sat there munching their pizza and talking with the Chef Whoopa (between whoops) while ignoring Pig. They didn't even offer him a taste of their pepperoni pizza. He offered them some of his but they looked offended and said no. Even then, they didn't offer him a slice. This combined with their harsh words had made him feel a bit of hatred towards them. Pig left them snoring in their beds a little after first light.

There's something magical about Rome before all the residents wake up. To be fair, there's something magical about Rome even after the residents wake. As Pig wandered the streets he was overtaken by both magical experiences. He saw an old woman scraping gum off the sidewalk in front of her stucco building, he was enchanted. It was a good thing, because Pig needed enchantment.

You see, the problem with Pig – and it's not an uncommon problem — was that he naturally assumed everyone liked him and wanted to be his friends. He had an affable nature. He was easy-going, somewhat intelligent, and while not overly interesting he at least got points for trying. That was how he saw himself: an internalized version. Other's looked at him and saw a guy who didn't pay much attention to his clothes, shoes, or hair. A guy who didn't care enough about himself to lose weight. A pudgy, not very bright, and not very interesting person who was eager to please everyone he met. The externalized version.

The sad thing is that these two people, the internal and the external, were oblivious to the each other's existence. If the internalized version had known of the external version, it would have been deeply hurt that people thought of it that way but would have done something to change itself. That way, it was more in line with itself on both the interior and the exterior. Now, don't get me wrong, Pig could look in a mirror and see what everyone else saw, but he was seeing it with all those internal qualities superimposed over the top of it. So, even though he was looking at the same thing, he wasn't seeing it.

The problem wasn't only Pig's. The problem was with people. People are judgmental and they tend to stick with the first impression made on them. The Hindus saw a chubby American who might be dangerous since his first impression on them was scaring the crap out of them by chasing them down the road. They were unable to let their guard down enough to get to know the internalized Pig and instead tried to keep the externalized Pig at arm's length. They would have refused to share a room with him, except since he had asked and been sent by the man from the hostel — they felt that a certain authority had placed them together and accepted it. Plus, they were very happy to have him pay part of their share.

Julian, being a bartender, was used to meeting people who projected a strong exterior but were insecure fools under it all. He made his career looking at the inner man and woman and so, he had seen the 'real' Pig and been able to ignore the unpleasant exterior most people got hung up on. Presumably, Melody and the Italian slut in Vegas had simply used Pig as a way to punish themselves. Inner loathing finding a slightly disgusting way of self-mutilating. And then there were the freaks...

People like Jenny who suffered from mental illness. Kal who was so fat and so black that he was used to being the oddity. Hi who was very cute, but suffered from a mental illness of her own. Hi feared the sun would turn her into her grandmother if a ray of it touched her skin. These people gravitated towards Pig. Like the lunchroom in those awful American coming of age movies. There is always one table where the freaky new kid is instantly accepted. The freak table where the kid with bright orange hair and freckles, the girl with scaffold-like braces, the fat kid, the non-athletic comic-book loving black kid, and the smartest kid in the school all sat together eating sandwiches from home instead of cafeteria food.

These had always been the people who wanted to be Pig's friends but Pig was as guilty of judgment as everyone else in the world. For all his life, he had avoided the freaks for fear of becoming one, unaware that he already was and there was nothing he could do about it. Pig consistently placed himself in groups of people who denigrated him, disrespected him, and made him feel bad about himself. He put himself among assholes and then wondered why people were assholes. Meanwhile, his natural cohort, the freaks were sometimes doing the same thing but sometimes having a wonderful time recognizing the diversity and wonder of the human existence.

The fact that Pig woke up with the idea to go search for Hi so they could get breakfast, explore Rome, and then meet up with Kai, the third freak, was an incredible step forward for him. One must admit, however, a big part of it was Hi was exceptionally cute and Kai had offered a free dinner. Still.. .this sort of progress is still progress. He was moving closer to the table filled with his own kind.

Rome is an extremely confusing city to navigate in. It took Pig two hours of going up and down the streets near Termini before he found Hi's hostel again. Going up the stairs, he felt like he was returning home even though he had never stayed there. Happy, clean, and bright-faced young people ready to see Europe on $50 a day.

Hi was in the reception area speaking with the clerk who, while American, spoke Japanese perfectly. When Pig walked in she ran to him, hugged him, kissed his cheek and said “Hi Pigu!” along with a lot of other things he didn't understand. The clerk did and was kind enough to translate.

“She says she's glad you made it back. She was worried about you. She thought the Hindus might be dangerous.” Since it reminded him, the clerk asked “Did you find the Hindus?”

“I did. Thanks. Do you guys have a dorm bed available tonight?” the clerk nodded.

“Sure, give me your passport and I'll fill in the details while you get some breakfast.”

After handing over his passport, Pig and Hi went through the hostel cafeteria and enjoyed the simple free breakfast. Coffee, juice, bread with jam, and corn flakes with milk. Hi jibber-jabbered to him in Japanese while she pointed out the various places they would visit using her guide book and map.

As I've said before, this isn't a travel narrative so I will skip over the visit to the Vatican, the many mansions and palaces, the stroll along the walls of the Papal City, through the ancient Jewish quarter, or the famous Villa Borghese. I won't trudge through the details of the Tiber River and the narrow cobblestoned streets surrounding it nor the Piazza Vittorio Emanuele. There is no need to describe the priceless works of art, the monumental architecture, or the sounds, smells, and tastes of Rome as experienced by Hi and Pig as they pleasantly traveled together with no language in common. Once or twice, there was something urgent that one of them would need to tell the other and at these moments they would duck into a cyber-cafe to use Google Translate to have a discussion. There were no smart phones in those days, but cyber-cafe's were plentiful.

An amazing world where two strangers with no language in common can step into a shop filled with people speaking a third language and find the means to instantly understand one another. While it's a cliché to say truth is stranger than fiction, the truth is in reality that the truth really is stranger. And that's strange in itself. Strange phrasing if nothing else. Humankind should be able to make fiction that is stranger than the truth but humankind rarely succeeds at such things.

As the day wound downward the two found a happy companionship. There was no need for the cyber-cafe when Hi said 'Waldorf Astoria' surrounded by a bunch of Japanese words and so they found a taxi, told the driver 'Waldorf Astoria' and set off to get a free dinner and see Big Kai and his Ukulele All-Stars.

Big Kai and His Ukulele All-Stars

The Rome Cavalieri Waldorf Astoria is one of the grandest hotels in the world. If Caesar had a palace and that palace was turned into a hotel for rich visitors to Rome, this would be the place. Lavish opulence, impeccable service, and a price that created expectation rather than a realization or pleasant surprise.

The taxi was met by three attendants. One to open the door for Hi, one to open the door for Pig and a third to take their bags from the trunk-of which, since they were staying in a somewhat gritty hostel in Termini, there were none. Walking the red carpet from the taxi to the revolving crystalline door they were greeted by three more attendants and upon walking in, a waiter handed them each a crystal glass of champagne. To be fair, before handing it to them he motioned towards a tray of juice or the sparkling flutes — there were choices for the well-heeled.

Inside lacquered furniture, oil paintings, and brocaded silks were as impressive as those in the Villa Borghese and the uniforms of the staff made Pig acutely aware of the fact that he was wearing jeans and a t-shirt which smelled like fetid sweat from walking around all day. Still, no one raised an eyebrow at the odd couple as they walked up to the concierge desk. That is where class can take you.

"Can you please direct us to the lounge?" Pig asked.

Now, the eyebrow of the concierge went up as if someone had pulled on a string attached to it. "The lounge, Sir? Surely you can be more specific."

Pig wasn't sure that he could be more specific. "Uh, it's our friend. He's doing a show tonight..."

"Sir, are you looking for the piano lounge, the jazz lounge, the opera lounge – though we mustn't call that a lounge, or one of the other lounges?" The eyebrow hovered there like a bumblebee.

Hi came to the rescue. Spouting a huge string of Japanese she took the attention of the concierge and caused him to turn to her. The eyebrow dropped from its judging posture down to what could be called the neutral position.

"Ah, yes," He said in English. "Of course the two of you are looking for Big Kai and his Ukulele All-Stars in the Tiepolo Lounge and Terrace." He pulled a map from beneath the counter that looked at least as large as the map of the Vatican Museums and probably represented an area bigger than the entire Vatican.

"You can take the courtesy shuttle to Eastern grounds and then you will need to walk through the Senate Gardens, past the Nero Nature Reserve, and turn left at the Da Vinci Exhibition Hall. From there you will go about 300 steps until you see the gilded stairway leading to the Tiepolo Lounge and Pool. You can catch the shuttle from outside here, " he pointed to a super-sized wooden door with gold fixtures and intricate scrollwork.

Hi set off directly and Pig had no choice but to follow. Through the door and they were on a narrow cobblestone track which wound through gentle green hills of grass. Pig wouldn't have been surprised to see golfers teeing up, so when the golf cart pulled up in front of them, it made sense.

This was no ordinary golf cart, however. It was jet black and the driver wore the classic chauffeur garb. He motioned for them to get in the back with his white-gloved hands and turned his head towards them "Where to? Sir, Miss?"

"Tiepolo Lounge and Terrace, please," Pig said while wondering if he was supposed to be tipping all of these servants. He had no idea. They had been here less than five minutes and already they had been assisted by ten people. He decided there were too many to tip them all, it would be unfair to tip a few, and besides, he was positive he would never come back.

The Tiepolo Lounge was gorgeous. For the evening's entertainment the usual brass candles had been replaced with tiki-torches and as a result the grounds seemed more welcoming and friendly than the rest of the hotel had. Not that the Waldorf Astoria was cold, but for someone from Vegas it all seemed rather –

untouchable. Not like the casinos where they expected everyone to gawk and touch things, priceless or not.

Kai, true to his word, had gotten them both on the list – Pigrone and Hiyumi, which sounded much better than Pig and Hi for these settings. There was no sign of Kai but they were brought appetizers, cocktails, and the view from the Tiepolo Terrace was spectacular. Pig felt as if he were watching a television screen as he looked down on the well preserved ruins and modern splendor of the greatest city the world had ever known.

The ground lights suddenly dimmed and the crowd's whispers drowned to a hush. The sound of waves lapping against the sand grew gently. Pig hadn't noticed speakers in the room, but the sound came from everywhere.

A deep voice began chanting in Hawaiian "*O Manu Hoi a Ka Pono Ne Ke Oi....*" After a moment, the chant was joined by a soothing voice, much higher pitched which spoke in English "From the land of Aloha comes the mission of love. A land of peace and abundance where the sun kisses the waves each day and the waves embrace the shores of Ha-VAI-ee." Suddenly there was the sound of an ukulele being strummed and a spotlight was directed overhead where Kai, dressed as an angel, slowly flew down from the ceiling. His hippopotamus body was clothed in white and the tiny ukulele pressed against his chest as he strummed. Because of his girth, his hands barely reached the tiny instrument well enough that he could play it.

Shocked beyond belief by this odd vision, it took Pig a moment to see the strained lines attached to pulleys on the ceiling or to recognize the titters and giggles coming from the tables around him. Kai was out of his element and judging from the smirks and whispered snide comments, this show was going to be a disaster.

Upon reaching the ground, an assistant ran out and unsnapped the cable from Kai's back. Kai walked to the raised dais in the center which served as a stage. The whole time his huge hands continued to strum the little guitar. Pig couldn't begin to imagine what kind of a flop this show would be. He sipped his cocktail nervously. Kai had been nice to him. It sucked to see him go through this. All through the lounge, people were watching and still whispering snide comments.

Kai sat and continued to play. His kielbasa-sausage fingers moved faster and faster on the neck of the ukulele while his carrot-like fingertips began to pluck complex rhythms from the instrument. The whispers died as the music rose upwards. Suddenly, no one was paying attention to the tiny feathered wings on the gigantic Hawaiian because all eyes were on his fingers and all brains were too busy trying to figure out how so much sound could come from something so small. There was no brain capacity left to think of witty insults in the face of such magnificent beauty.

The entire room was hushed; mesmerized as Kai's talent took control. The steps of the process forgotten with each note crushing out and glorifying the memory of the last. No one was thinking of a fat black man in a white angel suit now, no one was joking about the strength of the crane that had lowered him. Kai owned them. And then, he began to sing.

Somehow, the frenetic pace of the music stilled to a gentle rhythm. Like the sound of the waves crashing on the shores of Hawaii, the surprisingly high pitched voice of Kai began to sing "I see trees of green, red roses too..." The song was as unexpected as it was natural and the soft beauty of his voice, the tender feelings it evoked, the warmth that came through it — more than one of the guests found themselves brought to tears even before the introductory number was complete.

Rather than finishing completely, Kai segued into the next number as four very old, very skinny Hawaiians walked out from the four sides of the room wearing bright yellow togas covered with scarlet leaf patterns. Each of them held an ukulele, each of their voices joined Kai's and for those who were lucky enough to be there — truly a choir of angels sang that evening.

During the third song, Kai somehow managed to disappear, changed out of his angel costume, and reappeared dressed as the others in yellow and scarlet. It was when this song was complete that the music finally took a break.

"Aloha, Buena Sera, and Good Evening from the enchanted lands of Ha-Vai-ee," Kai said. "My name is Kailanianiole Mokapu Kaneshiro Mehele Kapaapononahuihui and these wonderful musicians are my

Ukulele All-Stars. Uncle Nappy Mohele, Uncle Rabbit, Uncle Pio, and the wonderful Auntie Lehua Kapaaponoahuihui – who I call Mom."

The room burst with applause. There wasn't a single person in the lounge who had not been touched by the music. "Before we continue, I want to tell you something about the instruments we play. They aren't Hawaiian. The tiny Portuguese guitar was brought by sailors in the 1700s and when Hawaiians saw them play they were amazed at how quickly the fingers moved. You know, in Hawaii, nothing moves very quickly except for the fleas the sailors brought with them. The word in Hawaiian for head lice is UKU and the word LELE means jumping — so the translated name of this instrument is really the 'jumping head lice' because the Hawaiians hadn't seen anything else that moved so quickly as those Portuguese sailor's fingers."

Kai's stories were funny and uplifting. By the time he and the Ukulele All-Stars left, there wasn't a person there who remembered seeing a fat man dressed as an angel being lowered by a wire and pulley. Instead, they remembered being transported to a different time and space and some of them were surprised to find themselves seated for dinner at the Waldorf Astoria instead of sitting on the shores of the Hawaiian Islands.

Kai and the All-Stars returned without their ukuleles. They now wore normal clothes. They circulated in the crowd and shared stories and jokes as people ate. Kai and his mother joined Pig and Hi at their table.

"Hey, I'm really glad you too made it. I don't meet a lot of people that I connect with, but I really enjoyed meeting both of you. Mom, these are the two I told you about from the plane. Pigrone and Hiyumi." Kai's mom was as skinny as he was fat. She had large laugh lines around her eyes and mouth. She shook each of their hands and said "Aloha."

"That was so incredible," Pig exclaimed. "I never thought...oh, I'm sorry...it's a pleasure to meet you Mrs. Kaia..." Pig had remembered his manners but couldn't remember Kai's last name.

"It's okay, Honey. Call me Auntie Lehua." she turned to Hi and the two had an excited conversation in Japanese.

Kai explained to Pig “Japanese is really the second language of Hawaii. Almost half of the people in our islands are at least part Japanese.”

At that moment, a waiter appeared. “Excuse me,” he said “Señore Pigrone Martin?” The waiter felt compelled to add the Señore since calling a guest Lazy Bones Martin seemed so wrong.

Pig nodded and the waiter continued. “I have a message for you here,” he indicated a folded card, “and you have also been requested to come to the Armani Suite. I can lead you there.”

Pig opened the card. “It's time to pay your blood debt. You will be given the package at Termini Station tomorrow at 8:00 a.m.” He was surprised to have been found, even though he had been expecting it, he had also been doubting it would happen at the same time. He was curious as to why they would call him to the suite and deliver the message though.

“Excuse me, was the note from the same person who is requesting to see me?” It had to be, but for some reason felt compelled to ask.

“No, Señore. The request was from the Contessa Albeezia von Hapsberg and she was quite insistent. She said to tell you that it was about Las Vegas. Please, I can lead you there now.”

“This shouldn't take too long, I'll be right back.” Pig said to Kai, Auntie Lehua, and Hi. He didn't know it was the last time he would see them for a long, long while.

The Contessa Albeezia von Hapsburg

Pig followed the waiter through the lounge, past the pool, down the hill, onto the green. At this point he was handed off to a second man who led him through a gallery, past a full service fitness center, and to a tarmac path where a third servant gestured for him to get into one of the black limo golf carts and then drove him across a vast campus of buildings, gardens, villas, and pools to finally arrive at a building that was like nothing Pig had ever seen. Even from a distance, it felt alive.

"What is that?" Pig asked the attendant.

"That, Señore, is the Armani Organic Living Space. We call it AOL. " the man's English was quite proper as if he had attended finishing school among aristocrats.

"Huh," Pig said aloud "And I thought AOL was dead." The champagne almost made the joke funny, but the servant didn't laugh.

"No, Señore, AOL is very much alive." While the statement could be taken a few ways, Pig had no doubt how it was meant because the building exuded life-ness. "The outer walls of AOL are made of artificial human skin generated though stem cells harvested from the sperm of undesirable donors who happened to have nice skin."

There was something about this night in particular when the magic of Kai and the Ukulele All-Stars had been invoked, a Baboobań blood debt had been called in, and for some as yet unknown reason he was being called to appear before a royal lady he had never heard of that made the explanation seem not only plausible, but utterly likely.

"Interesting," Pig said as they got out of the golf cart limo. He couldn't help touching the outer walls of the building as he walked past them. As his hand touched it, the wall twitched.

"The walls don't like to be surprised by cold hands, Señore, but if you stroke them lightly, the entire building exudes warmth and a feeling of well being." Of course it did...

They walked through the doorway. Rather than the marble he had seen in most parts of the Waldorf Astoria, the floors in AOL were made of thick, soft carpet. The attendant removed his shoes before stepping on the thick white pile.

"We shampoo the fur carpets weekly, Señore, but AOL doesn't like the feel of shoes against the skin. The fur is living as well, made using the same process as the walls but instead of human stem cells, these were the stem cells of Gustavo Armani's favorite cat. Sadly, the cat, Dr. Bumpkiss, didn't survive the extraction process but happily, he lives on as the ground floor carpet."

All of this was starting to feel very creepy. They reached the elevator and Pig was handed off to a fourth servant who showed him into the elevator and pushed the button for the top suite. The third attendant, like the others hadn't bothered to say goodbye.

"What's the elevator made from?" Pig asked, wondering what living parts had been used to create the elevator.

"I'm sorry Señore?" the attendant looked at him as if he were nuts.

"The elevator. What's it made of? Is it powered by amino peptides?" Pig was looking at it and while it seemed to be a very beautiful old fashioned lift contrived of brass and oak with an elegant control panel and iron grill worked doors, he was sure it must be crafted of some living thing to be in AOL.

"I wouldn't know, Señore." The elevator man said. "It would seem to be wood and metal. Ahem. We've reached the Contessa's floor."

The door opened to a marvelous room filled with rugs, artwork, and furniture that looked too expensive to relax in. A fire burned on the hearth directly across from the elevator; though across doesn't quite explain the enormous gulf that stood between the two. Two dark, leather chairs were pulled up to the fire with their backs to Pig.

"That will be all, leave now." The woman's voice sent chicken skin bumps over Pig's body and he was only too glad to step back into the elevator and nod at the attendant who only looked at him with a blank stare.

"Not you, Pigrone. You must come here and join me for a coffee." Pig stepped again from the elevator and felt the doors close behind him with a soft whoosh. He walked towards the two leather chairs and felt both excited and terrified as he realized who it was that had summoned him.

She was far more beautiful than he remembered. Slightly older but more elegant, more refined. Her jet black hair framed an olive complexion on a face that was accented by the bluest eyes he had ever seen, even though he had seen them before. She wore a green silk gown with a lazy ease that highlighted the perfect contours of her body while actually revealing nothing.

He didn't know what to say, but obviously she had no such hesitation.

"I told you what happens in Vegas, stays in Vegas, Pigrone!" the Contessa's mouth was perfectly formed as she spoke the words. "Why have you tracked me down? What do you want?"

Pig wasn't even sure how to begin so, as usual, he simply said what came to mind.

"You gave me herpes."

The Contessa's Story

The story she told him and the conversation they had was far more enlightening to Pig than one would expect from a random encounter with a nameless one-night stand that transmitted a virus that never goes away. And yet, in order to maintain the flow of the story and to catch the subtle details, it is necessary to depart for a while from Pig's perception of things. Unfortunately, he missed some rather important details because he was trying to see her nipples under the sheer of her gown and at other points simply because his mind had wandered away on some flight of fancy where he existed momentarily before being brought back to the Armani Suite by a delicious movement of thigh or a perfectly formed hand.

One can't blame him, but as the narrator, it is my duty to make sure you understand more about Contessa Isabella Marconi Albeezia von Hapsburg than her being another incredibly sexy woman of the Italian nobility.

She was born humbly in a 1959 Ford Cadillac when the vehicle intersected with an 1866 black walnut tree. The collision resulted in the death of her mother, Isabella Marconi – sole heir to the Marconi radio fortune and crippled her father, Juan Carlos Albeezia, a member of the Spanish Anarchist movement who had escaped Spain in the 1930s with not only his life, but also enough money so he never thought about any form of government other than capitalism ever again.

Incidentally, the chauffeur of the car in which she was born also survived the collision, but only long enough to deliver the child from its dying mother. Upon waking, Juan Carlos found the driver holding his infant daughter and his beloved wife dead. Taking the girl with one hand, the other drew the pistol and fired. Her first cries were silenced by a shot of revenge.

Juan Carlos doted on the girl and sent her to the most prestigious schools in Europe. Although not nobility herself, she was surrounded by the scions of blood and money from her first days in pre-school. Juan Carlos recovered from the accident with little more than a permanent limp, but he was never short of the means to hire someone to push him around nor the means to push others around if he so desired.

To his credit, he spared no expense on his daughter, though the messages she learned were a confused mixture of complete and total freedom for the self and complete capitalistic control of others in order to maintain it. Young Isabella was surrounded by opposing worldviews. On the one hand, the divine right of the nobility to enjoy the finer things in life and on the other hand the idea that no human had the right to control the destiny of another.

For Juan Carlos Albeezia, the solution was simple. On the surface he was a capitalist, industrialist, and member of the European elites. Below the surface, or by night if you will, he was known as the Spanish Godfather. Hated by the Italian Mafia but equally feared, he controlled huge swaths of Italian crime and was a force to be reckoned with. We could say that by day he found his marks and by night, he robbed them. Though saying that is a vast simplification since it was, in fact, his employees who were doing the robbing. His own hands were clean.

While he was guilty of hoarding a huge portion of the wealth he gathered, it amused him to use his ill-gotten gains for the benefit of those the gains had originally been swindled from. Not the blue bloods, but the common people. Thus, his crime syndicate siphoned huge amounts of capital into labor unions, trade organizations, housing for the poor, pension reform, orphanages, and the liberty of the common man from dependence on the government. In this regard, he had retained his anarchist origins — but, one would be hard pressed to remember that while watching him sip champagne and eat caviar on the polo fields each Sunday.

More amazing was that there were only three people who knew that Count Albeezia and the Spanish Godfather was the same person. Those people were 1) his butler 2) the Italian chief of his crime syndicate and 3) his daughter. Everyone else found no irony in Count

Albeezia discussing ways to reign in organized crime in Italy. However, as they say, that is another story and not meant for this narrative.

The origins of Isabella Albeezia von Hapsburg were unique. Her father's title was what we could call a 'courtesy' title given because he was the master of so much wealth. Her own was granted by charter when she married Count Otto von Hapsburg of Bavaria. The two met while attending the Sorbonne. For him it had been love at first site, as it was with most men (and many women) when they first met Izzy. For her, he was a means to claim the title she felt she deserved.

Their marriage was one of those storied weddings that young girls dream of and young men fear. The fear emerging from wondering how they will ever manage to give those young girls a wedding that will compare.Short answer, they cannot. The wedding was attended by the nobility of Europe and Asia plus more than a few notable African, North, and South American luminaries.

Over the course of the festivities, Isabella — the bride I might add, was hit on by no less than four dukes, three counts, seven princes, six lords, five movie stars, a president, a sultan, two kings and a dozen men and women of lesser standing. However, she only flirted with one and it was he that she made love to, while her bridesmaids giggled from the next room. She had banished them from her chambers when he appeared at her door an hour before she was to go to the chapel and be wed.

Her marriage to Otto was marred by three things. First, he was obsessed with biological construction and like many men of privilege, he devoted more time and money to his passion than passion to his wife. Thus the creation of Armani Organic Livingspace – called Dr. Ottostein's Monster by the staff at the Waldorf Astoria. Second, Izzy's ideas of anarchism extended to her body and so she was a constant cheat. While Otto was perfecting living carpet she'd perfected making love on bearskin rugs with men who weren't her husband. Third, she'd given Otto the herpes as a wedding gift and his outbreaks tended to be severe, painful, and almost non-stop.

For Izzy, the herpes had been her own wedding gift that kept on giving. Her pre-nuptial screw from the esteemed visitor to her bridal chambers gave her more than multiple orgasms. Izzy had spread this strain of herpes it across the world, often by pulling up to some drunk guy minding his own business and saying “Come fuck me, Pigrone.”

One should know, however, there was sentimentality attached to her. She had a tendency to pick up two types of men: those who were rich and famous or those who were handsome in a not quite tall enough, not quite thin enough, not quite enough hair way — in other words, men who looked like her late husband, Count Otto von Hapsburg.

So dear reader, you will hopefully forgive my narrative intrusion, but as you might guess, the Contessa wasn't willing to give Pig so much information. Instead she said to him.

“Herpes? My dear Pigrone. These herpes are royal herpes. Shared between the nobility of the world. Among the rich and famous, this particular strain of herpes is considered a mark of distinction. However, not one of them knows the origins... only I.”

“What is it?” Pig asked, oblivious to the fact she had told him it was a secret that only she knew.

The Contessa looked at him. There was more of Otto von Hapsburg in him than his almost handsomeness. There was a certain innocence, a child-like enthusiasm. She had thought of him often since dropping him at the International House of Pancakes on the Vegas strip. It was why she had been so shocked to see him in the lobby of the Waldorf Astoria.

“I will tell you,” she whispered, “but first you must fuck me Pigrone.”

A night with the Contessa was a night that could fuel the sexual fantasies of ten thousand men. In fact, that's probably how many the royal slut had slept with. Pig too, found her amazing, but since he had begun to have fantasies of women dressed in nun's habits doing his every whim...it was fairly tame by his fantasy standards. We must admit though, a night with the Contessa was filled with enough orgasms and champagne that he awoke with a start at 7:00 am.

He threw his clothing on with panic while the Contessa stretched like a she-panther in her bed.

“Don't go, Pigrone,” she mewed to him.

“I'm sorry but I have to. I'm going to be late and if I don't meet the Baboobans, I'm not sure what will happen.” Pig hadn't meant to tell her this tidbit of information but even so, her reaction was more extreme than he expected.

"Baboobans!" she said the word with so much energy and surprise that it momentarily stopped Pig from pulling on his left sock. She sat up in the bed and looked at him with suspicion.

"What?" he said to her.

"Pigrone. Did you say you are meeting the Baboobans? Did I hear that correctly? Why are you here? Who are you really?" She had pulled the silk sheet up and was staring at him with a look that he couldn't begin to fathom.

"It's complicated. I owe a blood debt." Pig pulled his other sock on while looking at her.

"But, I didn't even tell you... I mean... the herpes." There was a mixture of suspicion, tenderness, and a fierce something in her voice that again made him stop. This time in the midst of lacing up his right shoe.

"What about the herpes? What is wrong with you?" Pig was, as usual, genuinely confused since he couldn't see any relation between the herpes and the Baboobans.

"Pigrone," she said, looking at him intently. "The herpes were my wedding gift from the Sultan of Baboob. Mucho bin Mucho al Mucho. Em-Mucho himself."

While the news was fascinating, unlikely, and more than a little disturbing, Pig didn't feel he had time to waste considering the possibilities. "Contessa, I'm sorry, but I've got to be at Termini in less than an hour. I'm not sure what will happen if I don't make the appointment, but I'm not willing to find out. They know I am here and from what I hear, the Baboobans know everything."

The Contessa got up and moved to her dressing table. She opened a chest-like jewelry box and pulled a golden brooch in the shape of a marijuana leaf from it. The brooch was studded with rubies and diamonds and looked like something a successful rapper would wear on a chain. She held it out for Pig to see.

"Umm, yes, very nice," he told her as he looked for his jacket, "but I'm going to be late."

"You will take my limousine," she said. "However, you must promise to get this into the hands of His Majestic Eminence the Sultan of Baboob." She took the brooch and put it in a lavish red velvet box the size of a wallet.

"I don't know him, I probably won't see him..." Pig stammered wanting to accept the ride but feeling very afraid at taking such a valuable looking bauble.

"Of course you don't," she said. She was, however, more cognizant of Babooban customs and history than nearly anyone outside of Baboob and so she knew that at the completion of the satisfaction of a Babooban blood debt, it was customary to pay a visit to the Sultan's palace to leave a gift for the Supreme Smuggler. "I am sure that you will get the chance to pay a visit to him at some point during your stay. Now go, you mustn't make the Babooban Goons wait: that can be deadly."

Pig put the brooch in his pocket and turned towards the door.

"One more thing, Pigrone," the Contessa said as she grabbed him by the shoulder and spun him towards her. "You must never forget you carry the herpes of distinction. You are now marked as an important man and you should try to go about your adventures with more...confidence."

She pulled his face to hers and gave him a kiss he would never forget. Pig had kissed and been kissed by many women, but never before had a kiss felt so epic. Suddenly, he understood the feelings of heroes as they set out on grand, noble quests and were parted from their lady loves.

"Now go!" She shoved him towards the antechamber door where her servant had apparently been waiting. The door opened as Pig should have hit it. The servant took him by the shoulder and led him away. "He will get you to Termini on time."

Cloak and Dagger

The servant was a no-nonsense kind of man-in-waiting and he escorted Pig out the door, into the golf cart, to the garage, and into the limo faster than Pig would have thought possible based on his previous wanderings of the grounds of the Waldorf Astoria.

Once Pig was in the car, the man climbed into the driver's seat and turned to ask Pig "Do you have baggage, Señore?"

"Yes," Pig said. "At the Central City Hostel."

The tinted glass divider went back up and they were on their way. The traffic in Rome can be insane on even the easiest of days. The driver seemed to find roads with no lights, no lines of Peugeots, and no buses delaying them. In thirty-five minutes, Pig began to recognize the streets near the hostel and Termini. The limo pulled up in front of the hostel and Pig bolted out the door. The meaty hand of the driver caught his shoulder.

"That won't be necessary, Señore." The clerk came running out of the hostel carrying Pig's bag. The driver handed him a hundred Euro note and shoved Pig back into the limo with his bag in his lap. It was less than five minutes before they pulled up to Termini. The clock on the wall of the building read 7:59 a.m.

Once again, Pig bolted from the backseat, this time not being stopped by the driver. He turned his head with a grin. "Grazie Señore!"

The doors of Termini were blocked by touts trying to sell tours, private car hires, and hotel beds. Pig shoved past them and went into the building before realizing he had no idea where he was supposed to meet the Baboobans. He stopped, looking around. The place was its own planet.

How was he going to find them here? He saw three levels, high-end shops, McDonalds, cafes, candy shops, bookstores, buses to the left and trains to the right, commuter trains, metro and long distance trains all in the same direction but not clearly marked as to how to reach them. He began to panic.

In his head, he heard the Contessa's words. He was a man of distinction. He carried the Royal Herpes and in his pocket was a brooch worth more than everything he had ever owned. He was here, he had made it. The rest was up to them.

"I thought you would not make it or perhaps you might try to escape your blood debt."

Pig turned to find a tall man in a dark grey suit looking at him. The man had no long Babooban beard and looked like a regular Italian businessman, except he spoke with a clear American accent in perfect English.

"I am Mucho," the man said. He had chiseled good looks and was about Pig's age but far more successful, more handsome, taller, and more confident — but somehow Pig doubted that he had the Royal Herpes. This fact alone made it possible for Pig to face him with confidence.

"One doesn't run from an obligation, does one?" Pig surprised himself with the words. They sounded like nothing he had ever said before and aside from that, he spoke them with a British accent — for some reason. It must have been the herpes — or something.

"Well, I'm glad to see you here," the man said. "I don't like carrying this kind of thing for very long." He handed Pig a black leather attaché case.

"What is it?" Pig asked in a whispered voice.

The man smiled. "I don't know and I don't want to know. That is business between you and Master Mucho and no other man."

"What am I to do? Who do I take it to?" Pig needed to know something.

The man turned and walked away. "You will find your train and ferry tickets in the bag. A driver will meet you at the port in Tunisia. Don't miss them. Good luck."

The man disappeared in a swirl of Roman commuters who emerged from the metro. Pig desperately wanted to stop and open the bag but he was afraid of what the contents might be and he couldn't open it here in the middle of the terminal.

Seeing McDonalds again, he decided he deserved a break, though by any level of accounting, he had already received several. He stepped into the McDonalds, ordered an Egg McMuffin and a cup of coffee, and sat down at one of the tiny pressboard tables.

As he clicked the levers on the bag, the idea it could be a bomb occurred to him. The man told him he needed to get his tickets from inside though, so open it he must. No explosion. No bomb. Inside was a large parcel wrapped in black plastic. On top of it were his tickets. The train was leaving in six minutes!

Grabbing the tickets and snapping the bag shut, Pig rushed from the table leaving his McMuffin and coffee – but then, remembering them, he returned and picked up both. With his bag on his back, the attaché and McMuffin in his left hand, and the hot coffee in his right hand he quickly stepped out of the McDonalds to see if he could find the train to Civitavecchia.

After going down two escalators and running into the ladies room by accident, Pig found the train to Civitavecchia and boarded with thirty-seconds to spare. He had expected the conductor to be black and white like he was in all the old movies Pig used to watch on Sunday afternoons when he was too hung-over to go out but too awake to sleep. Maybe it was because Pig had lost his Indiana Jones hat and maybe it was because he didn't have an umbrella, but the conductor and everything else were in color and the train smelled slightly of urine.

Pig found his seat. He sat at a small table facing backward. The car didn't have many other people in it. He wondered how he would reach the ferry and if he should look at what he carried. Maybe he should get off at the next stop and leave the bag. An old man with a long beard and a dark complexion sat looking out the window midway down the car. Pig intuited the man was there to watch him. Suspecting that, he put the attaché on the seat next to him, stowed his backpack overhead, and ate his McMuffin. The coffee that he hadn't spilled while rushing to find the train had grown cold.

He was in a poke. That was all there was to it.

The African Ferry

The old man with the beard watched Pig intently for the entire journey. Pig felt trickles of sweat rolling down the back of his neck. He wanted to be anywhere rather than under the scrutiny of that old man. Pig stared out the window, tried to ignore the gaze of the other, but was unable. Finally, one hour into the journey, Pig stared straight into the old man's eyes and said loudly “What?”

The old man's eyes shifted slightly downward. He said nothing and continued to stare. Thinking of how he needed to 'man up' since he carried such important herpes, a priceless bauble, and he had slept with an honest to goodness Contessa – twice, Pig stood up and moved toward the man. The oldster said nothing, but used his hands to motion Pig downward to a sitting position. Stepping into the aisle, Pig noticed the old man's gaze was still firmly fixed on the place Pig had been seated.

Turning, he saw the video monitor which announced the weather, the next stop, and the line they were currently on. Apparently, the old man found staring at the screen more interesting than looking out the window. Hmmm....the screen said FR5 Intercity – arrival time 10 minutes. Pig looked back at the old man and saw that he was wearing a yarmulke. So much for him being Babooban. Pig hadn't heard of any Babooban Jews.

Back at his seat, he was unable to find the courage to explore what was in the briefcase. He still harbored an idea that the man was watching him, even though he had learned that he wasn't. As the FR5 wound its way into Civitavecchia, the views of the Mediterranean were dreamlike with castles built literally on the water. There was a huge sandy beach filled with bikini clad women — and men. Many of them wore only the bikini bottoms: both men and the women exposed their breasts for tanning. And yet the exquisite rounded turrets of the castle caused Pig to look away from the many boobies at the landscape. It was something Pig had never seen the likes of. Besides, as the old saying goes about tits, if you've seen one, you've seen them both.

The train went straight into the port area. Pig grabbed his bags and disembarked. The way to the passenger ferry terminal was marked with yellow arrows and without too much hassle, Pig found himself in the line to board the ferry. He'd expected to have some time to gather his thoughts but he was on a mad rush to his destination instead, with no time even for a sandwich. Pig expected the ferry to be a big, old, sinking, stinking, leaky rust bucket – especially since it was going to Africa. Pig carried colonialist imagery that denigrated the people of the world into caricatures. It was a product of his culture and education, but still it was ugly.

He pictured Africans carrying chickens and selling rice by the scoop on the decks. He thought the interior would smell like urine, have people sitting on rusty floors, and more importantly that there would be police moving among them, checking papers and sometimes hitting a luckless person with a lightweight baton. This was the kind of imagery Pig associated with taking a ferry to Africa.

Instead, he walked across a glass covered walkway into a plush velvet lined lounge that looked like it had come right out of the Stardust. Slot machines and a tall, mirror backed bar stood waiting for the moment the ferry was in international waters. Past the casino he found a cafe/lounge where a porter greeted him and asked to see his ticket.

The porter led him to a cabin. It was the size of a bathroom in a mid-range hotel. Just big enough for two pairs of bunk beds and an aisle between them. The two bottom bunks were already filled with the shapes of sleeping men despite the fact that it was only noon. Bags and gear had been left on every surface, including the bunk the porter indicated was Pig's. Pig lifted the clothing and bag that were on his bunk and put it on the opposite bunk. As he did so, he heard a squeaking below him and a shaggy headed white face peered up at him from the bunk below his "Why are you messing with my stuff, Mate?"

It was as Crocodile Dundee an accent as he'd ever heard. The man was nineteen or twenty but looked at him with an intense black gaze meant to be intimidating.

"This is my bunk," Pig said and for some reason aggressively added, "Now go back to sleep!"

The Aussie blinked in surprise, grunted, and rolled back over.

Pig heard a giggle from the other bunk and a second Aussie voice said from under the blankets. "That'll teach you to be a fucker, John."

Pig stowed his bags on his bunk, considered whether it was safe to leave them, foolishly decided it would be all right because the Aussies were there, and went out to find a sandwich. He made his way through five passenger lounges where films playing in five different languages, found three different food and drink stands, two bars, an indoor observation deck, and finally made his way to the outer decks with a sandwich, a bag of chips, and a beer. He was feeling wonderful.

Three flights of stairs led him to the top exterior deck where rows of wooden benches looked out at the port on one side and the Mediterranean on the other. The harbor itself was formed by two piers and a breakwater. It was filled with every type of vessel imaginable, from ferries to cruise ships to fishing boats to yachts to huge transport ships laden with Chinese cargo containers.

A large lighthouse stood on the end of the breakwater and while the heat and sun of the day were intense, it was enjoyable to stand on the deck, eat his sandwich, drink his beer, and watch the harbor traffic moving. The huge blue cranes pulling scrap metal from a freighter and dumping it into a huge pile on the shore was a sight that Pig had never before encountered. Life was beautiful.

He spent an hour on the deck then went below where he watched basketball in one of the lounges. After two hours on board, the ferry announced that it was commencing the trip. Pig found his way back to his cabin after getting lost in the maze of corridors and discovering that in addition to a chapel there was a Muslim prayer room, a children's play room, a VIP lounge which he was told he couldn't enter, and about four-hundred vending machines that sold everything from wine to sneakers.

Back in the room, Pig saw the fourth bunk was still unoccupied and noted that the two lumps of Australians seemed to have gotten out from under their blankets and gone out. He might have sat right next to them and not known them since all he had really seen was John's black hair and grizzled white face. He hadn't really had the chance to look at him though, despite his aggressive words, he had been terrified of a fight. Some of the Aussie's things had again migrated to Pig's bunk again. He put them back on the fourth bed so that someone else could sort them out.

It was the first moment he had been alone since Madrid. He decided it was the perfect time to look at what he was smuggling into Baboob. He grabbed the attaché, opened it and was surprised to find a note that hadn't been there before. It sat atop the black plastic wrapped package. "You probably shouldn't leave this sitting where someone could steal it — the contents are really quite valuable. And by the way, they are wrapped for a reason — so don't think about peeking at them."

Pig looked around but he was in a small ferry cabin, by himself, and to re-state the obvious, there was no one there — but again, quite obviously — there had been someone there. The note hadn't been there and referenced his leaving the attaché in the cabin unattended.

Pig snapped the case closed as the door opened up. A milk-and-coffee complexioned man walked in. He wore a white burnoose that matched the white turban on his head. In his right nostril was a gold stud and on his fingers were gold and silver rings set with stones that looked like they could be precious. His makeup was laid on with precision and the blush on his cheeks offset the blue eye shadow and heavy kohl around his eyes. The porter motioned towards the empty bunk covered with the Aussies' stuff and the man turned to Pig and put his jewelry covered hands backwards onto his hips.

"Is this your stuff?" he asked in an outraged voice as the porter disappeared and shut the door behind him.

"No," Pig motioned to the two lower bunks. The man began moving the things to the two bunks with no regard for what went where but appearing to want to distribute it evenly. As he placed the last bit up on John's bunk his eyes looked at Pig's lap and widened.

"Ohhhhh!" he squealed with delight. "You've got a very nice one. Can I touch it?" His hand was already plunging towards Pig's crotch.

Pig stood up in panic and the attaché dropped from his lap to the ground where the other man reached down to pick it up and stroke the outer leather shell.

"Oh, yes," he crooned, "this is exquisite." He looked up at Pig with those dark lined eyes from where he kneeled in front of him.

The door opened, the ferry jolted under way, and the second Aussie shouted out "Hey John, looks like we're sharing our cabin with a couple of nancies!"

The man in makeup stood up and handed Pig his attaché.

John poked his shaggy black haired head into the room and demanded "You guys been messing with my stuff?"

Okay Boomer

Pig felt odd carrying the attaché case with him everywhere as he wandered the ferry, but he didn't have an option. The Baboobans obviously had him under surveillance and as to the three men in his cabin, he didn't particularly care for any of them. The Australians were young, loud, and loutish and the Tunisian too worldly for Pig's simple tastes. Maybe colorful, flamboyant, and expressive would be better terms than worldly. In any event, he wasn't into it.

He wandered the many chambers of the African Ferry and found himself in the midst of so much exotic life and interesting scenery that he didn't mind not being able to lie down on his bunk in the stinky little cabin. There were plenty of places to wander but Pig found himself grabbing a length of wooden bench on the sun deck, sitting still, and watching the water and the distant land.

Many of the older European and American passengers had brought binoculars with them and were scanning the water and shorelines for marine wildlife. The obsessive scanning seemed neurotic to Pig who was content to sit and watch patterns form and reform on the surface of the water as the currents, waves, and other forces created a geometric mosaic impossible to contain and continuously reformed as fractals. These were better than the fractals on the visual setting of a Windows media player Pig used to stare at when he was stoned in Vegas.

The passengers on the ferry could be broken into groups. The Tunisian women and children were all in public lounges or children's play areas. The European tourists wore crisp clothing and were in their well-preserved 40's to 50's. The American tourists were older and looked slightly rumpled as if they had pulled their clothing from a suitcase. They wore clothing appropriate for golfing or the social hour at a senior citizens club. It wasn't the garb for travel in Pig's opinion .

They were in their 60's to 80's and sat in tight groups of four or more — usually two couples but sometimes an odd widow or widower. Next were the international backpackers who either sat with their packs next to them as if they expected to be robbed at any minute or had all of their possessions sprawled around them as if they were in a hostel dorm room. Many of these had laid out blankets or sleeping bags on the floors in less occupied corners of the ferry.

Finally, there were the Tunisian men who sat on the outer decks smoking and staring at the water oblivious to the no smoking signs all around them. Mixed among them was the occasional Italian man in a suit who joined them as a guest smoker.

Pig joined them after buying a pack of smokes in the snack bar below decks. They were happy to sell packages of cigarettes despite the ship-wide smoking ban. A pack of Marlboros cost him eleven Euro but he was happy to pay it since the idea of smoking while feeling the fresh Mediterranean air on his face appealed to him as an adventure in itself.

He didn't want to sit with the American senior citizens, so he sat on another bench nearby. It was a long bench. The left half was occupied by a couple of Tunisian men in stylish suits. They were obsessively smoking and exchanging the occasional word in Arabic between themselves.

To the right, backpackers had duct taped the corners of their tent to the metal deck and had retired into their nylon cabin. Heavy breathing and moaning sounds came from the bright yellow A-frame pup tent.

The benches at the rear of the deck were filled with sleeping backpackers and their gear. The benches closest to the water were filled with either Tunisian smokers or American seniors dressed as if they had gotten off a bus tour bringing them to the Stardust. A German backpacker played Madonna from his iPhone. Actually, Pig just assumed he was German because Germans love Madonna.

Such it was, on the deck. Pig pulled out his cigarettes, set the attaché case at his feet, and packed the pack as he had been taught to do when he was twelve by one of the security guards at the Tropicana. The idea was to have the tobacco tamped down inside of the cigarettes so that you could enjoy a more evenly burning smoke. He was aware of the looks from passengers around him as the pack went 'tat, tat, tat' against his palm. He pulled off the plastic, peeled back the foil, and removed a single smoke. For some reason, he had the urge to smell it, like a fine cigar. He decided not to resist the urge.

Putting the cigarette in his mouth, he lit it, inhaled, and felt incredibly privileged to be right there, right then. Life was pretty good as he stared at the varied blue water, exhaled the blue smoke, and felt the satisfaction of being someone, somewhere, doing something. He turned to see the angry blue hairs staring at him. Wait...why were they looking at him like that?

All over the deck, American senior citizens were staring at him with offended outrage. It couldn't be the smoking. The Tunisian men next to him were smoking and no one paid any attention to them, he saw Europeans smoking and no one seemed to care, some of the backpackers were smoking. Pig looked around to make sure there wasn't some kind of monitor or display above him, but found nothing.

Why in the world were they staring at him like that?

A chubby old woman with loose blue curls wearing a polyester blouse patterned with red, black, and orange squares along with a pair of white polyester pants stood up and marched directly to him in her orthopedic sneakers. She wore a determined busy-body expression on her wrinkled face and Pig imagined her hawk-like nose often prodded into the personal lives of other people.

“This is a non-smoking vessel!” She said to him in a clipped mid-west accent. “Perhaps you didn't see the signs, but I'm afraid you will have to put that out right now.”

Once again, he found himself not sure how to respond. The Tunisian men watched with interest, blowing smoke between the two of them and probably not understanding the words.

“Did you hear me? Do you un-der-stand En-glish?” she said with an exaggerated slowness. She said it again, louder when he didn’t respond because that always helps.

“Lady,” Pig replied to her after a moment's thought about what a hero would do. “I understand English fine, what I don't understand is why you're bothering me when 80% of the people up here are smoking.”

“I'm not bothering you at all, young man. I'm reminding you of your duty as an American. It's obvious that you're American and American's don't smoke any more. We follow rules. We're better than other people and we need to set an example. You are giving your country a bad name. How are these people ever going to learn manners and better behavior if someone doesn't show them? Hmmm?”

The material of her pantsuit was wrinkled, which Pig found odd. He thought Polyester wasn't supposed to wrinkle. He took another drag on his cigarette and thought about the Contessa, about those assholes Bing and Bob, about his friend Julian, about how many of the casinos in Vegas had changed to a non-smoking format, about how this woman had marched through life forcing her way of doing things on everyone around her. He looked around at all the aging American baby-boomers and saw that they too thought everyone should do things the way they wanted them done.

He blew the smoke in her face. “Okay Boomer.”

He kept smoking.

All around him, Pig heard enraged whispers. He took another drag. “You people grew up with parents who felt guilty about World War II, you got handed everything in life, you were never denied anything, and you raised your own kids as if they were your servants or some kind of insurance policy instead of the people who would inherit the world the world you set about destroying. You spent your lives raping and destroying. I've got news for you, lady. This isn't your country. This isn't your world. This isn't your ferry and this isn't your business. If you don't want to smell my smoke, go somewhere else, Boomer.”

It was the most eloquent speech Pig had ever given. Two tall baby boomers in pastel colored golfing shirts stood up and joined their hawk-nosed traveling companion. “You're going to put that cigarette out and apologize to this lady, sir. Do it right now or we have a big problem. We won’t tolerate age discrimination. We’re not minorities!”

Pig thought they sounded like they already had a problem. The two Tunisian men stood up. “This isn't America,” one of them said in very proper British English to the approaching baby boomers. “Fuck off.”

The smokers stood on one side of the yellow pup tent and the seniors stood on the other. It was a classic recreation of the age-old battle between East and West. It was the divide between the colonialist and the colonized. It was the shoot-out at the OK Corral. Pig's cigarette had become the symbol of the European and American boomer interference the world over. On one side — an odd mixture of post-colonialist Europeans, Arabs, and Pig. On the other side — the modern colonials: American baby boomers with angry-looking faces who believed their divine right was to be granted every whim and desire they might have before God would so unfairly end their glorious and self-meaningful lives.

The hawk-nosed woman screamed like the bird of prey her nose was reminiscent of. "I'm going to the captain! This is an outrage. We are Americans and even though we used to smoke, you have no right to make us breathe your smoke now that we've decided to quit!"

The two tall gold-shirt clad men stood on either side of her like linebackers in an American football defensive line. The one in yellow pastel smirked "Don't worry Karen. I'll be talking to the Italian consulate about this. He's a friend of mine."

The other scowled "We'll see what Silvio Berlusconi thinks about this when I write to him. I write very persuasively and my company does a lot of business with the Eye-talians. " He said it like that — Eye-talians.

The Tunisian man who had spoken up for Pig smiled. "Yes, wonderful ideas. By the way, my name is Abdel Wahed Fouazzi and I am the head of the Customs and Immigration department for Tunisia. My friend here is the Secretary-of-the-Tunisian-Interior. He doesn't speak much English. He and I are just returning from a conference in Rome where we smoked quite a few cigarettes with Silvio and the other leaders of the European Union. Did you know Berlusconi smokes? I assume he is a friend of yours too?"

The boomer's faces were less cock-sure than before. Pig heard several of them mumbling "I'm going to write my congressman" "You can't treat American's like this" "We helped to free your country" "You owe your freedom to us" "I will shut this ferry down" and other boomer threats as the assembled oldsters slowly disassembled and went below decks.

"My friend," Abdel Wahed Fouazzi said to Pig. "I have never met an American quite like you before. What is your name?"

"Pigrone Martin," he answered, acutely aware of the fact that the attaché at his feet was filled with some sort of contraband and he was talking to the head of Tunisian Customs and Immigration. "Is it true you are coming from a conference in Rome?"

"Yes, yes. It is never an easy thing to rebuild a country," Fouazzi replied. "Oh, I am glad to meet you Sidi Pigrone. I had begun to lose hope in America because of these fucking boomers." Fouazzi took his hand and then embraced him kissing both cheeks and then pressing his lips fully to Pig's. "You will be my guest in Tunisia, Sidi Pigrone."

The moaning from the pup tent reached a fever pitch and everyone left on the deck sat down to watch. They all began to smoke again. Smoking on a ferry. Who knew it would lead to so much good will?

People of Influence and Power

For the rest of the journey, Abdel Wahed Fouazzi and the Secretary-of-the-Tunisian-Interior were never far from Pig's side. The two men had both been low-level bureaucrats in pre-revolution Tunisia. Both had been chosen from among their peers to ascend to power during the post-revolution. Their rise was based on their education, standing within their departments, and the amount of money that their families contributed to the new revolutionary government. The Secretary-of-the-Tunisian-Interior was one of one-hundred-and-twenty-seven new secretaries, eighty of which shared names with the previous secretaries.

"It is a fact of life," Fouazzi explained to Pig, "that the more things change, the more they stay the same. In the Arab world, people have become used to certain families with certain names holding a greater share of the political power. While there are always new names that arise with any revolution, in a few years you will see people with names like Hussein, Gaddafi, or Bushad wielding power again — though perhaps never at the level they did before."

Pig was trying to understand. "But, I thought the whole point was to get democracy so that people could make the best choice from the best potential candidates. Isn't that the idea?"

Fouazzi laughed. "That's the idea people who hold the power would like those who grant the power to believe. Think about it — neither I, nor my friend were elected. In your own country, it is the same. Do you vote for judges? Did anyone vote for Karl Rove? Did anyone vote for Dick Cheney when he was made the Secretary of Defense or George H. W. Bush when he was put in charge of the CIA?"

Pig understood, but didn't like the way it made him feel. He felt the greasy nauseous feeling that comes with the knowledge of an unpleasant truth.

"Appointments are made to consolidate power and solidify allies who would otherwise cause problems. From within those appointments, a proving ground, if you will, players of the great game get the chance to prove themselves and their ability to build a base of support among the powerful. For example, in your country, a junior congressman gets elected by the people. In turn, he appoints and hires those people who will most benefit him — the children of donors to his campaign become pages and interns. The brother of a helpful senior congresswoman gets a plum position as an attaché or media relations aide. And so it goes... one of those interns might be the next junior senator or figure out that he can rise faster if he expands his usefulness. Eventually, you have a guy like Karl Rove writing the policy for the President of the United States or a guy like Dick Cheney selecting himself as the best candidate for Vice President."

"How were you selected for your position?" It was a rude question, but Pig felt it was okay in the context of the conversation they were having.

Fouazzi laughed. "I was selected because I speak seven languages, was educated at Harvard Law School *and* Oxford, and because I am intimately familiar with the trade and customs policies of not only Tunisia, but also of most of Europe, the USA, Japan, China and the rest of North Africa. And, most importantly, my sister is married to the first General of the Tunisian Armed Forces who sided with the revolutionaries. All of my brothers were given positions, all of my brother-in-law's family was rewarded with contracts or plum jobs, and so you know I'm not making all of this up about power, my father was the former Minister of Justice under the old regime but has now retired quietly to a country estate where he still pulls strings. To answer your question in a nutshell, I was chosen for this job because I am the most qualified for it on many levels." He mocked himself but held his dignity higher with his words and honesty.

"As to my friend here..." Fouazzi motioned to the Secretary-of-the-Tunisian-Interior. "His father is the richest man in Tunisia. He was educated in Cairo and holds a Master's Degree in Irrigation. Obviously, he was also the most qualified for his position, too. This is the Tunisian custom and tradition and it is the same throughout the Arab world. Democracy is a necessary illusion to keep the people in check — we provide them with a choice among the candidates we select and they are provided with the comforting illusion of choice... but, wait, am I boring you?"

Pig was embarrassed. He had drifted off watching the ferry move closer to a big island. While listening to Fouazzi, he thought about his attaché case and continued to wonder what kind of contraband was in it. He wondered if Fouazzi would make him disappear into a deep, dark pit when he discovered it. Still, he was listening and so he jumped back into the conversation when he heard Fouzzi's question.

"No, no. It's all very interesting. Thank you for explaining. Is this Tunisia?"

Fouazzi looked at the blocky concrete buildings behind white sand beaches and shook his head. "No, we won't arrive in Tunis until tomorrow morning. This is our last stop in Italy. This is the port of Pozzalo, the southernmost point of Sicily and of Italy. From here we go to Malta and then onward to Tunisia. This city is famous because long ago, they say an entire convent of nuns was abducted by Tunisian pirates and were used to...well, never mind. We will have several hours here. Will you join us ashore for some dinner?"

Without waiting for an answer, he turned to the Secretary-of-the-Tunisian-Interior and spoke rapid Arabic with him. Then he turned back to Pig.

"Come, we know a wonderful place where we can get dinner near the port."

"But, I've already gone through passport control," Pig said.

"My friend, rank has its privileges and when you have friends with some rank, the world opens up to you." Fouazzi smiled. "Don't worry about immigration or passports. You're with an international delegation now. Let's get some seafood."

It was that easy. They walked from the deck to the boarding plank and the Secretary-of-the-Tunisian-Interior flashed a special document inside his passport. Fouazzi explained something in Italian and they walked through customs and immigration without anyone even asking to see Pig's paperwork. He still carried the attaché' and from time to time wondered if anyone would ever ask him what was in it. So far, so good.

The restaurant wasn't far from the port and had a view of cargo ships and containers being unloaded. The jetties of the harbor jutted towards the Mediterranean and Pig could see the lanterns of fisherman sitting still on the quais. Other lanterns bobbed up and down in rowboats. The interior of the restaurant was aged red laquer decorated with cliché relics of the seafaring past. Anchors, lines, diving helmets, aquariums, and nets along with wooden oars, paintings of lighthouses, and three statues of Neptune brandishing his trident.

The waiters wore tuxedos that looked like they had been purchased in the 1950s. The lighting was red. It was a red light fish house. The two Tunisians ordered huge amounts of food, bottles of wine, and smoked constantly — even while eating.

"I thought Muslims didn't drink," Pig asked.

"Important Muslims don't drink when other Muslims are watching," Fouazzi said. "Why? Are you a Muslim?"

"No, I'm not, but I had heard that."

"Good," Fouazzi said, "Then we don't need to worry about it anymore. To Muslims!"

The three men raised their glasses and continued with their Sicilian seafood and wine binge. The process of getting back on the ship was as uncomplicated as the process of leaving it, though all three men were quite drunk.

"Meet me on the sundeck next to the pup tent in the morning," Fouazzi told Pig. "You will be my guest in Tunisia – but please, make no mention of the wine when you meet my mother."

Back to his cabin, Pig found John and the Tunisian curled up in one bunk and the other Australian sprawled halfway onto the other. He moved all three of their belongings off his berth, kicked aside an empty bottle of whiskey on the floor and was asleep before his head hit the pillow.

The sound of the intercom announcing they were coming into Tunis woke him. Since he'd slept in his clothes, leaving was a matter of picking up his pack and the attaché case and then making his way up to the pup tent on the upper deck. The brisk morning air was slightly warmed by the smell of garbage burning. He found the two Tunisian men looking as crisp as the morning. They didn't look as if they'd had a single drink the night before.

Fouazzi spoke on his cell phone and when Pig heard 'American' mixed in with the Arabic, he wondered if the conversation was about him. Pig was learning to roll with the punches through the fog of his hangover and the fog that lay over the harbor of Tunis.

This was going to be an interesting morning.

Manners and Customs of the Tunisian People

If it hadn't of been for the alcohol, Pig probably wouldn't have slept. He might have come up with some sort of plan to escape from the two Tunisian officials. Instead, there he was, a smuggler bringing unknown contraband into Tunisia and walking down the steps of the ferry with the man in charge of the people who would bust him, beat him, and throw him into some deep dark well where no one would ever hear from him again.

As he followed Fouazzi and the Secretary-of-the-Tunisian-Interior down the metal steps to the auto deck, he considered escape from them, but one was in front of him and the other behind. There was no getting away. He was already in their custody.

Except that he wasn't. On the auto deck, Pig saw a tour bus filled with the American blue hairs. As he and the Tunisians filed past on the narrow aisle between vehicles, the American oldsters stared out the windows while holding cameras and binoculars at the ready to see whatever they might. There was nothing to see or take pictures of in the auto hold, but they were ready.

On the side of the bus was a picture of a mousy looking man with straw blond hair and wire glasses. He wore a tan windbreaker and a serious smile. Pig wasn't surprised the angry baby boomers were on a Rick Steves' *Africa through the Back Door* tour. He was beginning to see the symmetry of experience in life. He didn't understand it yet, but he was becoming aware of a process that is always the first step towards understanding. Pig had changed, even if he didn't know it.

Fouazzi gave the angry boomers a jaunty wave as he walked by the bus to a black Lincoln Navigator with dark tinted windows. The vehicle 'beep beeped' as the Secretary-of-the-Tunisian-Interior pressed the security button on his keychain. Fouazzi opened the back door of the vehicle and pulled a small red bag from under the seat.

"Please, get in and make yourself comfortable." He smiled at Pig and despite the sharpness of his teeth, Pig felt comfort because there was friendliness in the smile. Fouazzi opened the small bag and removed five small flags which he snapped into place at various points on the vehicle. He climbed into the front seat next to the Secretary-of-the-Tunisian-Interior, who apparently had no problem driving himself around.

The ferry gate lowered so the vehicles could proceed and all of the drivers revved their engines as if they were getting ready to race. Armed soldiers walked onto the vehicle deck from the loading dock. They held their weapons at the ready as they stood in front of the other two rows of vehicles. One of them motioned for the Navigator to move forward.

Pig would have driven out slowly and carefully, but the Secretary-of-the-Tunisian-Interior gunned the engine and they shot off the ferry and up the ramp like a bullet from the soldiers guns. Pig saw a broad grin on the man's face as they rapidly picked up speed moving down the jetty.

Fouazzi said something that sounded harsh and demanding. The Secretary slowed the vehicle and parked at the customs and immigration station on the land side of the pier. Instead of using a parking space, he pulled into one of the vehicle lanes and shut down the engine.

"Come with me," Fouazzi said to Pig as he got out of the car. "Bring your bags."

They walked into the cold, white concrete building and Fouazzi flashed his badge. He greeted each official they encountered. Most of them sat behind bulletproof glass windows. They stood and saluted when they saw him. They smiled obsequiously at Fouazzi and buzzed he and Pig to deeper and deeper levels of the Arab bureaucracy.

As they proceeded into the bowels of the building, Pig became more and more nervous. This was where things could turn ugly for him. It was too late, there was nowhere to run, no way to get away. He was trapped.

They reached a wide corridor where a long concrete desk separated twenty clerks from those who would soon be passing through. The immigration counter.

"Give me your passport," Fouazzi said to Pig.

Pig pulled it from his jacket pocket and handed it to Fouazzi. Fouazzi handed it to the immigration agent on the other side of the counter and asked. "What is the purpose of your visit to Tunisia?"

"I'm going to Baboob," Pig said even while realizing it might not be the right answer and then wondering what the right answer was.

The entire room erupted in laughter. Men and women in crisp bright blue uniforms roared with laughter in the damp humidity of the underground room. Some of them repeated what he had said while shaking their heads. Fouazzi laughed with them.

"You are full of surprises," he told Pig, while looking around the room and catching various clerks eyes to share their merriment. His look said to them "Can you believe how funny my friend is? Isn't this guy great?'

"Not many people know enough about Tunisian culture to joke with us, but seriously, what is the purpose of your visit to Tunisia?" Pig had no idea what the joke was, but was thankful for a second chance.

"Tourism," he lied.

"Great, we need more of the right kind of tourists." Fouazzi motioned to the clerk in front of them. The man stamped ten papers with rapid motion, put stamps on three others, filled in Pig's name and passport number on yet more papers, placed stamps on them, and then rapidly used another hand stamp with a 'thwack, thwack, thwack' to stamp on top of the other stamps, the signatures, and anything else he had written. Finally, he stamped the blank page at the back of Pig's passport.

Fouazzi took the passport from the officer and handed it back to Pig. He then surprised everyone by jumping on the counter-top where he addressed the officials with a little speech that Pig didn't understand a word of except for being certain that he heard 'Americans'.

At the end, Fouazzi beamed at the agents and said in English "... and now, my friend and I are going to Baboob!" Again the clerks and agents erupted in laughter.

"Come with me, now we search your bags." Pig didn't feel like laughing any more. They marched down the white cinder block corridor to the next big chamber where stern looking male guards, canine units, and very tough looking women in pale blue uniforms with red stripes down the legs sat around playing cards, drinking coffee, spitting, and smoking. To be very clear, the men smoked and played cards. None of the women did, but they all spit and drank coffee.

They walked to a conveyor belt x-ray machine where Pig put his bags down.

"What are you doing?" Fouazzi said to him, "Come on."

A muscular man with the shiniest black boots Pig had ever seen approached. He began shouting at Fouazzi. Fouazzi shouted back. The two men each became more and more red faced and Pig realized he was in the midst of a serious problem. The big man reached for Fouazzi's hands. Fouazzi responded by thrusting his hands upwards and knocking the shiny black billed officers cap from the big man's head.

The big man's hands reached for the pistol at his side, but before he could reach it, Fouazzi pulled a knife from somewhere it had been concealed. He placed it under the big officer's chin ready to drive it upwards and kill the man in an instant.

The officer slowly raised his hands. The room was quiet enough that Pig heard a fly buzzing in some distant corner. There were many guards there, watching silently. As the man's hands went upwards, the corners of his mouth turned up with them.

As quickly as that, the knife was gone and the two men were embracing and kissing one another on the cheeks, the hands, the top of the head, back on the cheeks, and on the lips. Both men spoke in Arabic at the same time, not listening to each other but going through a ritual that was expected and necessary among Arab friends who have not seen each other for a long while.

A plate-glass window looked out to the vehicle lanes where the black navigator and the Secretary-of-the-Tunisian-Interior both sat waiting. The Secretary-of-the-Tunisian-Interior was smoking and drinking coffee in the vehicle's open door. He was nodding his head with the rhythm of the music he listened to, but the glass wall was soundproof so not a sound made it into the building.

Fouazzi and the big officer finished their ritual of greeting and warmly held one another's hands. Fouazzi turned to Pig "This is my cousin Khalid. He is the most dangerous man in Tunisia," Fouazzi laughed. "Well, the second most dangerous. He is my chief of customs and duties. Usually he is not here, but he knew that I was returning today and came to surprise me. I think I surprised him instead."

Pig nodded as Fouazzi told Khalid about him, speaking Arabic and motioning to Pig. The speech went on and on. Pig was certain of three phrases this time... first of all 'going to Baboob' — which caused Khalid's eyes to widen with surprise and a mirthful grin to appear on his face. He slapped Pig on the back good naturedly. Next, Pig again heard 'Americans' and finally he distinctly heard 'Rick Steves' – Khalid's face became more serious.

Fouazzi turned again to Pig. "Are you carrying any contraband?"

Pig didn't want to lie but he didn't want to tell the truth so he took the middle ground. "Not that I know of."

"Okay, let's go," and that was it.

The three of them walked out the glass door to the navigator. As they passed the canine units, the dogs went berserk. They lunged towards Pig. The handlers looked at Khalid with questions on their faces and then looked at Pig with more questions. Khalid simply shook his head. They walked out the door as the Rick Steve's bus pulled up.

"This is where it gets fun," Fouazzi said. "Do you want to know how long those American boomers are going to be here?"

Pig looked at him, wondering what the question meant.

Fouazzi went on. "They are going to be here for the next twelve hours. During that time, four of them will disappear and the rest of them will be unable to locate them. Don't worry, they will be fine, but this will be a very expensive stop for them. It's not often we get to have this kind of fun."

The bus stopped and it's door opened . Customs agents swarmed the bus. Khalid embraced Fouazzi and then shouted orders at his men. They opened the baggage compartment while officers with dogs walked around the vehicle, looking under it with mirrors held on long poles and herding the scared looking passengers towards the immigration doors. The Secretary-of-the-Tunisian-Interior was bobbing his head to loud Arabic rap that spilled from the Navigator. He returned Khalid's perfect salute with a lazy one and a smile before going back around to the driver door. A black suited man came from inside the building and the Secretary-of-the-Tunisian-Interior allowed him to open the rear driver side door for him. Now they had an official driver.

As he watched the boomers get herded and harassed, Pig felt no satisfaction. He felt guilty. Maybe he should have put his cigarette out and let the chubby lady boss him around. In a way, this was his fault. “They won't be hurt?” he asked.

Fouazzi smiled at Pig with genuine understanding. “They may have their pride damaged, but no, they won't be hurt. You see, we are going to make them show prescriptions, search through all of their baggage, find problems with their passports, and make them worry, but we won't hurt them. In fact, we won't even really charge them very much money... but they will have to deal with a lot of smoking. By the way, how did you know that when Tunisians want to say something is none of your business, we say we are 'going to Baboob'? I've never met a foreigner who knew that before. Remarkable and full of surprises.”

It took a moment for the implications to fully hit Pig. He had told the immigration officer who asked him why he was visiting Tunisia that it was none of his business. Because of who he was with, he had been passed through customs and immigration without any problems. Watching the dogs, mirrors, and blue hairs — he realized how lucky he was.

“Going to Baboob,” he said, mostly to himself, but Fouazzi laughed again.

“Yes, I know, but really, I will get the secret out of you yet!”

Abduction

The professional driver who replaced the Secretary-of-the-Tunisian-Interior drove with a quiet assurance that had been lacking from the richest man in the country's son. His acceleration and deceleration were smooth, he didn't jerk on the wheel when he wanted to make a turn, and he drove like a man whose job was to drive people safely to where they were going. Not like a rich kid who didn't care if he ran someone over.

Pig had a million questions he wanted to ask and a million fears swirling inside of him. What was inside the case? Had he really blundered across customs so easily? Was this some sort of cosmic pay-off for standing up to a pudgy hawk-nosed militant-non-smoking baby-boomer? How was he going to get to Baboob from Tunis? Why did the Tunisians say 'going to Baboob' as a way of saying it was no one's business?

The landscape of urban North Africa rolled by out the windows of the vehicle they rode in. The vehicle, by the way as an odd fact, cost more than the combined annual income of the first seven thousand Tunisians they passed. Pig stared out the window while the two men made calls on their cell phones. There was garbage everywhere, piled in the streets, filling any vacant space, and drifted against the sides of dirty concrete buildings. Not a landfill or dump, but more like a stiff wind had picked up the entire contents of a landfill and evenly distributed it over the entire city. Dented red taxis wove in and out of traffic that was equal parts pedestrians, bicycles, donkey carts, and automobiles.

To Pig's eye, the clothing of the people looked as if half of it had come from the Salvation Army and the other half from the wardrobe of Lawrence of Arabia. At one stop light, beggars came to either side of the Navigator. One of them wore a dirty grey t-shirt that had a picture of a cat with a magnifying glass on and said "Pussy Inspector." The other wore a long black robe and a small knit skullcap. They stood with hands out and knocked on the windows of the vehicle. Each of them were ignored and left behind when the light turned green and the traffic surged forward.

The intersection wasn't clear but the vehicles simply zigged around those vehicles left behind in the cross traffic like water going to either side of a stone placed in its path. The eddies of Tunis traffic trapped a wizened old man in a well worn black suit who drove a donkey cart. He was stuck on an island of cross stream flows, but no one paused to let the man reach the safety of the other shore. He would have to wait, but of course, he would be the first to reach safety when the flow was switched: if he didn't get trapped by someone else or run over before the light changed again.

Women in black burkas with nothing but their eyes showing walked nonchalantly down the street. In some cases, the skin around their sunglasses was all they revealed. They walked hand-in-hand with their children down rubble strewn sidewalks where filthy dogs soaked lazily in the shade of abandoned looking buildings that were obviously still fully inhabited. The ebb and flow of the traffic revealed the outline of a mosque rising above the city and an army of smaller minarets in every direction. Concrete art-deco architecture mixed with urban slum. Neither looked as if they had been painted in a thousand years – except for the mosques and the rare modern office building standing like a stranger in a strange land. These stood proudly with shining concrete and steel rising above the street level graffiti that covered their lower regions.

Pig had been expecting to see minarets that looked like rockets – since those were the only ones he had seen before. The stylized mosque towers at Aladdin's Casino and Resort were based on those of Mecca and Istanbul. Instead, the mosques of North Africa sported square towers like the battlements of an English castle, each with a small, square, green-tiled roof on top. A sword hilt was thrust in as a weather vane at the tops.

Soon, they were out of the slums and into wide, palm tree lined avenues that stretched for fountain-studded miles. Flower gardens broke up the roadside and wealthy looking pedestrians occupied the sidewalks. Gucci, Omega, Prada, Louis Vuitton, and Apple Stores lined the boulevards. It could have been the area leading to the Mall of Las Vegas.

The garbage was gone, the urchins were gone, the graffiti was gone. Uniformed police stood in pairs at every corner watching every move made by those who were there. A street car looked like it had come directly from San Francisco as it moved smoothly up the hill in front of them. The passengers hanging out the doors and windows were the only sign this wasn't California or Nevada.

“This is the new Tunisia,” Fouazzi said to him with pride. “It's brand new and was built in the past five years in an attempt to steal some of the tourism from places like Morocco, Turkey, and the Emirates. We spend more money keeping this area safe for tourists than we spend policing the rest of the country combined! There's a Hilton, a Radisson, and a Ritz-Carlton and you will find every major brand in the world available here. This is the Beverley Hills of Tunisia.”

It was impressive, but for some reason, Pig felt ill as he looked out the window at the landscape. It had changed so drastically! He saw two policemen pull a poor man from his bicycle. They dragged him off the street. The bicycle lay where it had fallen until a teenager darted from somewhere, jumped on it, and rode off quickly with worried looks over his shoulder.

The car moved into an area of high walls and manicured gardens. Here, there were few if any pedestrians and the view through the metal gates of the villas and estates revealed opulent grounds, tennis courts, swimming pools, and palatial buildings. In the space of three blocks Pig counted twenty-seven security cameras. Those were only the ones he saw.

The driver pulled into a drive, beeped the horn, and two guards came running out to pull the security gate clear. The vehicle was known. Pig wondered about the human power being used on the gate when an electric motor and remote control would have been easily within the budget but could only discern that the use of human power had always been a signal of prestige. It was like the story of the Empress who insisted on using slaves for a foot-stool. “Anyone can have a normal foot-stool,” she had said. Subservience sent a message.

"This is the home of the Secretary-of-the-Tunisian-Interior," Fouazzi explained to Pig. "We will have dinner here this evening and then go to my family's country estate in the morning. For now, you are the guest of the richest man in Tunisia. You are in the safest place in North Africa. If Gaddafi, Hussein, or bin Laden had been here, they never would have been taken! They have their own missile defense system." Pig didn't know if he was joking or not.

Liveried servants ran out to the vehicle as it pulled in. The driver parked under an ornate Roman arch next to a villa that would have looked at home in a Vegas casino. Pig saw uniformed Army troops patrolling the perimeter of the walls. They carried snub-nosed machine-gun pistols. A guard tower stood some distance away. This wasn't a villa, it was a fortress.

"Are those private security?" Pig asked Fouazzi as they got out of the vehicle.

"Of course not," Fouazzi winked. "Tunisia protects its most valuable citizens at all costs. At least until the next revolution."

Inside, there were a million Salaam-a-leycums said between the two men and the three women who came to meet them. The women were dressed in western styles, wearing no veils, and looking like anything but what Pig thought of as Muslim women. He was introduced to the mother, grandmother, and sister of the Secretary-of-the-Tunisian-Interior.

Each of them had the ageless look of Hollywood stars that pay for the most cosmetic of plastic surgeries. Full pouting lips filled with Botox, no wrinkles, full silicon bosoms, perfectly styled black hair with blonde highlights, and thick black eyeliner around perfect green eyes that may have been brown but covered with contact lenses. Pig thought he could determine which was the sister, but had no idea which of the other two women was older than the other. In fact, it was possible the one he thought was the sister was really the grand-mother.

A flurry of activity surrounded them while the introductions and greetings took place. The kisses and excited chatter of the three women kept the Secretary-of-the-Tunisian-Interior occupied for quite a while. Fouazzi pointed to a servant standing next to Pig.

"Abdel-Latif will show you to your room so you can shower, change, and have a rest. Meet me here in two hours. I want to take you on a small tour of Tunis. There is much to see here."

Not quite knowing what to say, Pig said "Okay. See you later."

Abdel-Latif led Pig to an elevator which took them up one floor. He was led down a carpet-lined hallway to another palatial room filled with uncomfortable furniture that cost a fortune. Abdel-Latif put his bags down next to a bureau, showed him where the towels were, indicated the restroom and the bed, and left without a word.

Pig needed a rest. He needed a shower. He was glad to have the opportunity. Dropping his clothes on the floor, he walked into the marble shower and turned the brass taps until hot water steamed around him. For the next twenty minutes he soaked in steam and scalding hot water until he felt that his skin had been washed away.

Wrapping a soft, fluffy white towel around himself he stepped back into the bedroom as a black sack was thrown over his head and two people knocked him to the ground. He hadn't noticed they were there, but he noticed he was falling and the lights had suddenly gone out. He never actually saw the two people.

Mucho

Pig struggled but it did no good. He was bound and gagged with the black hood still over his head. Not only that, he was rolled up into the bedspread and then, rolled up even further in the room's carpet. Being Pig in a blanket, he had no way of knowing he was being rolled up in the expensive carpet he had been dripping water on, but in fact, that was the case.

Now, as the narrator of this story, it's important that I remain a neutral third party and don't become involved too much. I understand this. However, it's important for you to know that we weren't at all upset about Pig getting the carpet wet. After all, it wasn't our carpet, so it didn't particularly matter — but, it was important to get Pig out of the family home of the Secretary-of-the-Tunisian-Interior – so we used the carpet.

Dammit. Now, I've done it, I've spoiled my third person perspective. Suddenly and without warning I've dropped into this tale and made it a first person narrative thus breaking nearly every agreement between she who tells the story and they who read it — but wait, there is still time. We can continue as if nothing happened, so I beg you dear reader, please ignore my ugly faux pas and continue reading from the third person perspective — at least for the moment.

Pig struggled, but bound and gagged, rolled and stuffed as he was — he was unable to struggle very effectively and quickly gave up. He thought about the security of the compound and wondered who his captors might be. He imagined he was in the hands of Tunisian rebels, but the possibility existed that he was also in the hands of the new Tunisian government, since, as Fouazzi had explained to him, he was in the safest compound in all of the Middle East and North Africa – still, he wasn't feeling very safe. In fact, he felt incredibly vulnerable as he was jostled and jounced out doorways, down stairs, over a wall, and into a waiting truck.

Not only was he stuck, but Pig was feeling short of breath. He was hooded, wrapped in a blanket and then rolled in a carpet before finally being thrown into the back of a truck so it's no wonder his constricted brain decided to lower the amount of oxygen he was using to the absolute minimum and shut down all non-essential functions. Like the Greek, Spanish, and Italian governments, his brain decided to enact strict austerity measures until a new agreement could be made with his lungs about the amount of oxygen that would be distributed to the rest of his body. In other words, Pig passed out.

He was unconscious for most of a long bumpy sixteen-hour ride. He had no recollection of the things he would have seen if the truck had windows, if he wasn't rolled in the carpet, if he wasn't rolled in a blanket, if he hadn't of been hooded and gagged. Of course, being all of those things, if he had been conscious the entire trip would have looked something like this:

{silence}
{darkness}
bump!
{darkness}
{silence}
roll! bump! roll!
{darkness}
{silence}
-repeat-

So, it is fortunate that neither Pig nor the reader is forced to endure sixteen hours of that. As to what was really going on...well, for the moment, we also have {silence} and {darkness} because the next thing that Pigrone Martin knew, he was being licked by a big fluffy dog.

His brain decided to lift the oxygen austerity measures once oxygen revenues had been resumed. The restrictions had been lifted by the rug being unrolled, the blanket being unwound, and the hood and gag being removed. He opened his eyes and looked into the sad brown eyes of a Saint Bernard as it looked down at him with its dinner-plate-sized paws on his chest. In a panic, Pig looked for the attaché case and found it handcuffed to his wrist.

He was in a one room cinder block cabin that had three long narrow windows. The windows were high off the floor and there was a corrugated metal door held closed with a piece of chain hitched onto a nail. He heard people moving around outside and wondered if the dog standing with its paws on his chest was dangerous. From the look in its huge brown eyes, he couldn't believe it. She looked like Nana from Peter Pan.

"Down girl," he said as he tried to sit up. Nana, since she had no other name to call her by, stepped back and allowed him to rise from the canvas cot he was laid out on. He stood and walked towards the door. It nearly smacked him in the face as it was kicked open from the outside.

"Unbelievable! Absolutely unbelievable!" The man entering was in his twenties and wore black commando garb. He looked like a ninja except for the huge black beard hanging almost to his waste. A big knife in his belt gleamed wickedly and there was something familiar about him though Pig was certain he had never seen him before.

"Is this the way you pay a blood-debt? You put yourself and my grandfather's cargo into the hands of the people we are trying to get it past? Are you insane or stupid? Now tell me, how did they capture you?" The man spoke quickly with a curious accent that was like nothing Pig had ever heard before. The G's were harsh and the R's were trilled, the rhythm of the words started high and then descended so that each sentence felt like it was going to explode only to calm itself before the next verbal assault. The pitch of the man's voice was high and then low and while Pig was reminded of Hindi English via Bollywood films, at the same time he was sure the lyricism was Spanish and the lazy glamour of Italian was there as well. He was so completely and utterly confused by the entire setting and situation that he stood there thinking these things while the angry young man stared at him fiercely.

"Well, say something. How did they capture you?" Yes, there was definitely something familiar about the man.

Pig decided it was best to explain. “I was taking a shower at the home of the Secretary-of-the-Tunisian-Interior and when I came out they grabbed me. I didn't see a thing but I felt...”

“Not us, you idiot. The Tunisians – how did they capture you? Did they nab you going through customs? We saw the mess there this morning — crying old people, calls to consulates, the American Ambassador coming down to try to find people who had gone missing. Not to mention the absolutely insane way they tore through people's luggage. Our man onboard feared for his life and actually stowed back on rather than risk coming through — that must be it, they got you in customs.” The man sounded as if he was convincing himself of something he was completely uncertain of.

Pig allowed him to go on. “Our man lost track of you when you left your cabin. We knew you'd turn up somewhere, but it was quite a surprise to find you being held in the home of the Secretary-of-the-Tunisian-Interior... how did he get you?”

None of it made any sense to Pig. These were his captors, these were the ones who had taken him, kidnapped him, bound and gagged him. And yet, here he was being interrogated by this man who didn't seem to know anything at all. Who was this?

“Who are you?” It seemed like the best place to start.

The man laughed and swelled up his chest. “Me, Señor? I am Mucho son of Mucho, son of Mucho, brother of Mucho al Mucho bin Mucho, grand nephew of Em-Mucho himself — descendant of Hasan i-Sabah and someday perhaps, a great man myself. In other words, I'm Mucho. Salaam a leycum.” He was holding out his hand for Pig to shake it.

“Oh, Salaam a leycum to you too, Mucho. I'm Pig.” At some point, he had begun to think of himself as Pig, like everyone else did. He wasn't exactly sure where that had been. “Mucho, you're Babooban?”

“Of course I'm Babooban. My name is Mucho. Didn't you see my knife and my beard? What did you think that I'm Tunisian or something?” the fierceness had completely left Mucho.

“Why did you kidnap me?” Pig asked.

“Kidnap you? What are you talking about? We rescued you. We saved you from torture and probably from death. Kidnap?” Mucho sounded outraged now. Outraged and proud.

"Well, I was taking a shower. I was supposed to have dinner with the family of the Secretary-of-the-Tunisian-Interior – hey what's his name anyway? Oh, well, doesn't matter – I was supposed to have dinner with his family and then Fouazzi and I were going to..."

"Fouazzi?" Mucho spit. "The dog son of dog parents and the most corrupt man in all of Tunisia, the worst of the worst and definitely the most dangerous kind of ....ptaaah!" Mucho spit again.

"I thought he was quite nice, he helped me get through customs and was going to introduce me to his mother, though I think he probably smokes and drinks too much for a Muslim, but that's really none of my business..." the lack of austerity on his oxygen supply was making Pig drunk with the abundance of the delicious O2. Words spilled out of him in a far greater flow than he usually allowed.

"The man is disgusting. He simply won't take a bribe. His customs agents have been brainwashed into thinking it is their duty to tax illegal imports instead of taking cash bribes, he is a travesty, a blight upon the face of the earth. The curse on Baboob. He was going to introduce you to his mother? He took you prisoner and was going to introduce you to his mother?" Mucho sounded incredulous now.

"No, no, no. I wasn't a prisoner at all. He was helping me, he's my friend." Pig wasn't sure that he should have said that but the 'f' word had already escaped his mouth before he realized he had aligned himself with the curse on Baboob.

"Impossible," Mucho said to him. "Our man on the boat said that the Americans were all involved in a smoking dispute with Fouazzi. He lost track of you in Sicily but heard from the purser that you had been taken ashore by Tunisian officials. We assumed that you didn't come back on board because our man didn't see you again — did they fly you to Tunisia?

Pig was also completely confused. "Your man on board. Oh, of course, the one who left the note in the attaché. Hey, who was that anyway? No, they didn't fly me. We went and had dinner and then came back. I left the ferry with the Tunisians."

"You stayed in their cabin?" Mucho asked. "Yes, of course, you must have, otherwise our man would have seen you. That explains it. They snuck you back on board, locked you in their cabin and then drove you off in their vehicle. That's why our man didn't see you return to your cabin."

"No, I returned to my cabin. Your man got it wrong, by the way, who was your man on board?"

"No, impossible, he would have seen you. He was in the same cabin. There was no way you could have snuck past him."

"Your man was one of the Australians? Was it John?"

"Australians? What are you talking about? Our man was Tunisian – although it might be a stretch to call him a man, still, despite his life choices, he has always been very reliable and he said you never returned."

Pig laughed despite the seriousness of his situation. The Tunisian – it was brilliant. "The Tunisian was Babooban?"

"No, of course not," Mucho said. "There are no gays in Baboob, but there are tons of Arab homosexuals and since they are persecuted by all the Arab governments, they don't mind working for us from time to time. It's ridiculous, all the Arab countries refuse to even believe that there are homosexuals in their countries. How stupid is that?"

Pig sensed an illogical syllogism or something along those lines in the statement, but now wasn't the time to argue about it ... or even point it out.

"Listen," Pig said. "When I got back to the ferry, the Arab was passed out. He'd gotten hammered and seduced one of the Australians – I think. When I left in the morning, they were still cuddled up, I..."

"Oh that bitch," Mucho said. "You can't trust the gays. You can't. They're damaged goods, they'll lie and tell you what they want to hear. Of course — that's why she...he...stayed on board. Dammit!"

"So anyway," Pig continued. "Fouazzi helped me get through customs and actually, the whole American tour problem was my fault because I refused to put out my cigarette and by the way, I think you are wrong about him. I think he's a good man."

"The gay?" Mucho asked.

"I don't know about gay, but Fouazzi is a good man." Pig decided it was right to stand up for someone who had stood up for him. He was coming dangerously close to no longer being a douchebag.

"Of course he's a good man. That's the problem. He's a very good man and the last thing we want is a good man in charge of customs. Understand? He wants to put a tax on everything. He won't take bribes. Ptaaah." Mucho spit again. "Did he know what you were carrying? Did he see the product?"

Pig hadn't even seen the product.

"No, he didn't. What is this anyway? Do you have a key for these handcuffs?" Pig lifted the attaché case. Nana the Saint Bernard who had been sitting and watching the entire conversation patiently now gave a short bark as Pig lifted his arm.

"Oh, right. Sorry about that. We didn't want you to be separated from it. Sorry but we left your pack and personal stuff back there, but we did grab your clothes." It was only then Pig realized he was still wearing nothing but a white towel. His clothes hung on steel nails driven into the cinder blocks and his hiking boots were on the floor. He moved to his clothing and began to dress. Checking the pockets of his trousers, he found his passport and money still there.

Reaching into his coat pocket, he found the expensive Bauble the Contessa had asked him to deliver and it reminded him of his promise to do so.

"Mucho. You're really the grand nephew of Em-mucho? Am I going to get to meet him?" Mucho ignored him.

"If you weren't a prisoner, why were they holding you captive?"

"Captive? I wasn't a captive. I was a guest."

"Dammit. Those idiot women. They destroyed an important node of our intelligence network for nothing. Are you telling me they weren't holding you captive? You weren't a prisoner?"

Pig was frustrated. "Of course not," he exploded. "I've been telling you. They were my friends. I was a guest!" A thought occurred to him, "Am I a prisoner now?" He was buttoning up his shirt.

"A prisoner? What? We rescued you, idiot. I mean, we thought we were rescuing you. We were trying to help. My grandfather said he liked you so he wanted us to give you assistance now and then."

"Your grandfather?"

"Yes, Mucho."

"Aren't you all called Mucho?" Pig asked.

"Yes, but he's the only Mucho who serves Pickle Juice Tea in Madrid."

"Master Mucho of the Pickle Juice Tea is your grandfather?" Pig asked. He was putting the pieces together as he pulled up his socks.

"Yes, of course he is. Why else would we help you?"

"And you said your grandfather's brother is M-mucho?" Pig tried to justify the image of the bent over old man with the very sharp knife as the crown prince of a tiny nation. He had thought he was a struggling immigrant.

"Yes, weren't you listening?" Mucho seemed unfairly annoyed.

"And so I'm smuggling something for the Crown Prince of Baboob who told you, his grandson, to rescue me from my friend the Secretary-of-the-Tunisian-Interior?"

"No, you've got that all wrong. He didn't tell *me* to rescue you. This is the first time I've ever seen you. He told me to pick up the package that Fatima left in the cabin."

"Who's Fatima?" Pig asked.

"Which Fatima?" Mucho replied.

"You said Fatima left a package in the cabin."

"Yes, but the package wasn't really a package, it was you," Mucho explained.

"I understand that, but who is this Fatima who left me here. How did she get me? Why did she leave me here?"

Mucho looked at him with an amazed expression. "Fatima is the one who rescued you, idiot."

This was going nowhere fast. Pig decided to change course.

"Are we in Baboob now?" Mucho's look hadn't changed, he still was looking at Pig like he was an idiot.

"Where are we?" Pig asked.

"We're in the Tunisian Mountains about ten kilometers from Baboob."

"Great, let's go then. Do you have a car?" Pig was tired of this back and forth.

Mucho laughed. "A car? What good would that do. Don't you know the reason Tunisians say 'going to Baboob' when something is none of your business is because there are no roads that lead there? You have to sneak into Baboob. It's the only way unless you are Em-

Mucho, and then you can use your helicopter. If you're sneaking someplace, it's probably nobody's business, right? So, that's why they say it."

"Yeah, but Em-Mucho is your grand uncle, right? So certainly you can call him or something? Right?"

"Are you crazy?" Mucho asked. "Who the hell ever heard of calling Em-Mucho to help a smuggler settle a blood debt? That's the stupidest thing I've ever heard."

"How do we get to Baboob?" Pig asked. "You're going to help me, right?"

Master Mucho of the Pickle Juice Tea's grandson Mucho smiled as he said "You're going to ride my ass." And with that, he turned his backside toward Pig and stepped out the corrugated metal door and into the sunshine.

The Sacred Asses

Pig watched the man walk out the door wondering why he'd never been into guys. Was it genetic? He followed Mucho out the door where he found the man adjusting the gear on two small fuzzy pack animals.

"Which ass do you prefer?"Mucho asked him while motioning to the two donkeys. "Rumsfeld is more comfortable but Rove actually is more efficient."

Pig could hardly tell the difference between the two. They were the smallest donkeys he had ever seen. Each of them barely reached his waist and they had fuzzy patches of hair that looked like toupees sitting between their long ears. Sad brown eyes stared from their faces and bulky saddles were strapped on their backs.

The African Wild Ass is often mistaken for the common donkey or burro when seen from afar, but is a much more hardy animal. This fact is attributed to its small size and stubborn nature. While no one has been able to prove it due to the refusal of the African Wild Ass to cooperate with scientific studies, it is commonly thought that the African Wild Ass can carry twice the load of the common donkey or as much as five times the load of a horse when one factors in a ratio of weight to payload. It is for this reason and others that in the Sultanate of Baboob, the ass is considered sacred.

One thing no one has figured out is how best to ride them. Babooban's developed an innovative harness that allows the rider to sit side-saddle with their legs dangling to one side. This sometimes causes problems for the novice ass-man who may be tricked by the air filled bellies of the ass as the saddle is being cinched. At the first dangerous opportunity, the ass will deflate its belly with a loud belch and send its rider hurtling toward the ground. On the pathways to Baboob, this is usually a fall of several hundred feet because of the ass's propensity for belching on narrow mountain trails.

Mucho was no stranger to preparing an ass. As he came toward the first ass, which was called Rove, Mucho gave it a hard kick in the stomach which caused a super-sonic belch to escape from the beast. Mucho pulled the saddle cinch as tight as possible. Rove's big sad eyes looked even sadder but Mucho didn't take the time to feel bad. Instead he gave Rumsfeld an even harder kick to the gut and repeated the process.

"They're sacred animals but tricky," he explained to Pig. "They'll kill you for their own reasons and you'll never see it coming. It's not easy to be an ass-man in Baboob"

Pig was relieved that the animals were there since it saved him from making awkward excuses. After a brief introduction to the riding styles for African Wild Asses and a few words of caution about letting Rove have his head, the two men sat side-saddle on the beasts. With a rounded pommel thrust up between their legs, they began the final leg of the journey to Baboob.

"Does everyone use the same trail?" Pig asked, wondering if they would encounter anyone along the way.

"No, of course not." Pig was certain he knew the look on Mucho's face even without seeing it. "Each family has its own secret way of getting in and out. While there have sometimes been crossovers or odd encounters along the way, for the most part the path to Baboob is a quiet and reflective journey where one can think about the profits, consider the dangers already encountered, and dream about eating goat balls on Friday."

"I'm sorry," Pig said. "What was that last part again?"

"Goat balls. Every mother in Baboob cooks goat balls on Friday and no mother makes them better than my own. She roasts them first, then cooks them in a secret sauce, serves them over rice, and, well, of course you will have to join us. My mother's balls are the most delicious balls of them all."

"Yes," Pig murmured. "Sounds wonderful."

The land around them was lit by the bright light of a full moon. Scrub oak crawled up gentle inclines and shallow ravines stretched off like the fingers of a giant had tilled the rocky ground around them. Small palms grew from piles of rocks and thistles poked out in every direction, already dried as if waiting for some interior decorator to come along and place them in fancy vases to fulfill a Vegas mansion's southwest theme.

Pig felt as if he were heading down into the Grand Canyon, something which he had never done, but which he had often imagined. Never mind that he was heading upwards. Never mind that he followed a man he had just met into a country from which no road emerged. It still felt like he was one of the Brady Bunch kids heading down into the canyon with Mike and Carrol. He could almost imagine Indian's hiding behind the rocks ahead of them or Milton Berle with a dangerous tiki — but that was the Hawaii episode.

The landscape was enchanting. They came to a small stream, the vegetation became more lush, and the sounds of the water jumping off the rocks added a merry element to the otherwise somber journey. Mucho lifted his leg and stepped off of Rumsfeld while Pig did the same with Rove. The two asses pushed their snouts into the water and began to slurp noisily

"We will arrive after sunrise," Mucho said. "It is likely we will encounter some sort of a Tunisian patrol along the way. Your friend Fouazzi is trying to set up an actual border and regulate trade and exchange between our countries. The Tunisians though are fairly lazy and usually have a big fire burning, so we shouldn't have any problem with them. The harder part will be evading the Babooban Customs and Immigration Agents."

"Are they dangerous?" Pig asked.

"Dangerous? Of course they are. If you give them the chance they will take every item you carry, arrest you, charge you a fine, and then humiliate you when they release the failed smugglers each Saturday. They are swine," he looked at Pig, "no offense."

"Oh, none taken," Pig said. "How do we get past them?"

"We bribe them."

"But didn't you say they will take everything? Why should they take a bribe?"

"It's like this," Mucho explained "If they think they are getting something for nothing, they are quite happy, but if you give them the chance, they will take everything for nothing, do you understand?"

"Not really."

"Well, lucky for you, you don't have to understand. Do what I tell you."

"Okay." Pig was relieved that understanding wasn't required since he found himself utterly confused.

As Mucho had said they would, they encountered Tunisian border patrol a short way down the trail. Five men sat around a huge fire, drinking tea and laughing at stories that despite the Arabic, sounded to Pig like typical man stories of women and prowess. There was a tone to it he recognized.

"They are blind," Mucho whispered. "Come."

The two men led their asses around the perimeter of the Tunisian border camp and were soon well away from it. It was another two hours before Mucho motioned for Pig to bring Rove to a stop.

"Shhhh. They are not far away. Get off the ass now. Do you still have your attaché'?" Pig held up the bag which was still handcuffed to his wrist. Yes, he still had it.

Mucho put his mouth to the ear of Rumsfeld and whispered into the shaggy beast's ear. He then kissed it on the snout before moving to Rove and doing the same thing.

"We will send the asses to the customs agents. They will think we have died along the trail or been seized by the Tunisians and then we can slip away into Baboob."

"But, isn't there a better way than to let them take your ass?"

Mucho smiled. "No, my friend. My asses are special. They earned their names. There is no better way, but don't worry. No man has ever tamed my ass and yours is just as dangerous." Mucho loosened the cinches around the bellies of the pack animals. "Rumsfeld and Rove have been responsible for the deaths of more men than you can imagine. They are tricky and not to be trusted. In fact, they may arrive home in Baboob before we do."

"They kill people?" Pig hated to sound so incredulous, but he had a hard time imagining these two sad looking asses as dangerous killer animals. "Don't the custom's men work for your grand-uncle?"

The whispered conversation had lasted too long, but Mucho kindly took a moment to explain things. "The customs men are those Baboobans who have been too lazy or too stupid to make it as smugglers or craftsmen. It is the job of last resort for those who can't do anything else. To put them out of their misery is a mercy. Besides, it's their own fault."

He smacked the asses of the asses and motioned for Pig to follow him. They crawled up a narrow ravine and a short time later heard the triumphal shouts of several men. "They have found the pack animals."

"What was in their packs?" Pig asked.

"Rumsfeld's packs are filled with expensive silk from Persia. Rove carries Beluga caviar from Norway, chocolate from Switzerland, perfume from France, and sunglasses from Italy. It's an expensive cargo, I'm sure they are very excited to have found it."

"Aren't you sad to have lost it?"

"No," and that was that. Mucho turned and climbed up a narrow iron ladder bolted into the jagged face of the cliff. Letting the attaché case dangle, Pig followed. The ladder was placed in such a way that it was invisible unless one stood directly in front of it. Pig wondered how many smugglers had passed this way before him.

He'd thought of himself as a smuggler for the first time which was a hallmark moment if there ever was one. He deserved a card but there was no one to give him one.

They climbed up cliffs, swung across ravines on ropes, crawled through narrow tunnels and finally emerged on a steep mountain face that looked towards the imminent sunrise. Across a wide valley, Mucho pointed to a thin band of trail which wound along the contours of the opposing cliffs. Pig heard the jangling of harness straps drift across the divide and then he saw the two men sitting on the Baboobаn asses.

The asses moved slowly, picking their steps with care to avoid loose talus. To step in it meant tumbling to their doom on the ragged boulders below. Mucho put his fingers to his mouth and blew a shrill whistle that echoed across the valley. It was followed by the excited chatter of the two border and customs agents. The next sound was a roar as the two donkeys expelled air-cleaving belches which allowed the loosened saddle packs to slide sideways and sent the two customs agents to their deaths. Pig couldn't make out where they had landed but the hollow 'thunks' followed by no sound but the continued jangling of ass harness told him everything he needed to know.

A violet light filled the sky and as if on cue the voice of a hidden Muezzin called out to let the Baoist faithful know that it was now the time for prayer

It was the most beautiful and tragic sound Pig had ever heard. Partly this was because it was coming right after the feelings that welled up in him as he watched the two men die. Compounding things were the emotions that rose as he realized he had almost fulfilled his quest, and the triumph that seemed to radiate from the sun as it once again rose successfully over the dark of the world as it always had and always will.

"Allah hu akbar," Pig said.

"Yes, he's the greatest," Mucho said excitedly, "Come on, we're almost there. We can have breakfast at my mother's."

Pig followed his new friend and idly noted that Arab mom's must be much better mothers than his own.

Turban

As he walked into the city of Turban for the first time, Pig knew it was different from anywhere he had ever been. He wasn't *exactly* sure what it was. Everything about it was different, but there was a feeling he could sense but not identify. Blocky mud brick buildings rose all around him and wood smoke came from pipes thrust out at forty-five degree angles from second floor walls. The windows were set high and too thin for a person to fit through. The streets on the outskirts of Turban were little more than wide mud tracks.

It was very early, but there were already Babooban people moving through the streets: roundish, frumpy women in colorful mother superior garb carrying long flat boards with the days baking on them to the community ovens in the center of each neighborhood. Young men with the peach-fuzz of adolescence proudly sported on their faces carried large buckets of water from community wells. Old men wearing long, distinguished beards of grey and black moved away from the nearest Baoist mosque to their homes, returning from their dawn prayers to their lives of elderly devotion.

Few of the buildings were painted. Turban itself blended into the ground beneath it, a neutral sand tone broken up by the whitewashed walls of Baoist mosques and the occasional stained glass window. As they moved into the city the roads narrowed until there was scarcely room for three men walking abreast to move on the narrow ways.

Mucho grabbed Pig roughly and pressed him against a wall as two donkeys came around the corner behind them and nearly ran them down. The donkeys didn't stop, but Pig was sure it was Rove and Rumsfeld sans their most recent riders.

"Aren't you going to stop them?" Pig asked.

"No, they know the way home and no one will try to take them here inside Turban. Piracy happens outside of Turban, but here in the city, there is a code we all adhere to."

Pig thought of the two men, lying dead at the bottom of the canyon. "What about the families of the custom's men? Won't their wives or children be missing them? What will happen?"

"It's simply the way of things, my friend. Custom's men never have wives or children. No Babooban woman's family will allow her to marry a man who hasn't successfully smuggled or learned an important trade. How could he provide for a family if he can't even accomplish that? No. Those men won't be missed. People will think they emigrated into Tunisia, where about anyone can get married. It's the way of the world; the weak and the stupid among the rabbits are the first to get eaten."

For Pig, it was not so easy to forget the deaths of the men. He stopped speaking about it, realizing he had come against a cultural wall that would not be penetrated. Life had a different meaning here. People were more concerned about donkeys than other people in Baboob.

And that was when he became aware of exactly what the big difference was he'd sensed in Turban. There were no cars. He couldn't hear the sound of engines, there were no cars, no sidewalks, no beep beep beep of a car door being opened, no sound of garbage trucks, no sound of a van backing up with more beep beeps, no beeps or honks of horns. No cars parked on the curb, no driveways, no garages, no motorcycles, no scooters, and no airplanes overhead.

It was a profound difference. One that Pig had never imagined. One that floored him.

"Mucho? Aren't there any cars in Baboob?"

Mucho turned to him and grinned. "In Baboob? Yes. We have some cars. I lied when I said there are no roads. Of course there are a few. However, Turban is a sacred city. There are no motorized vehicles allowed within its borders. There are no electric blenders, no saws, no lawn mowers, no weed-whackers, or anything else that would disturb the sense of the holy here. Turban is a city of peace. A place where the first Em-Mucho retreated to escape the chaotic world and where that world is kept at bay. Welcome to my city. Welcome to my home, my friend."

As they turned the corner the street narrowed again. They came on a crumbling hovel. Walls had fallen in, timbers of the outer rooms had collapsed, and the door made of vertical cedar logs was hanging on one leather hinge. Large walls topped with broken glass surrounded the ruin and beside the door stood Rumsfeld and Rove. The two asses filled most of the narrow alleyway.

Mucho smacked Rumsfeld on his rump and the beast moved forward pushing Rove with him. Mucho lifted the wooden door out of the way, pulled a key from his pocket and unlocked a heavy metal gate that had been hidden behind the door. He gave a quick whistle and the two pack animals backed up, pushed through the doorway, and disappeared.

"And now it is your turn," he motioned for Pig to enter the interior of the ruin. Pig hadn't expected Mucho to live in a ruin. As a nobleman and the son of an important family, he had expected luxury, but perhaps the family had fallen on hard times. He stepped through the drab, crumbling doorway pushed past a black cloth curtain...

...and entered the world of Arabian fantasy. Ornate colored tile and polished metal filled every surface that wasn't covered with flowering plants or intricately woven rugs. A shiny brass fountain stood in the center of an open courtyard that was tiled with colorful geometric shapes of stars, rectangles, and diamonds. Along the edges of the wall were thick cushions wrapped in plush velvet buried beneath soft looking upholstered pillows in greens, reds, blues, whites, and yellows.

Tall wooden doors were open across from him and inside the room opposite, Pig saw silk tapestries, polished wooden furniture, displays of museum quality antiques, and row upon row of books. The carved plaster ceiling of the room looked as if it had taken millennia to form in the dark of some hidden cave. Looking up, Pig saw the sky from the center of the courtyard. Rising above the blossoming orchids and plumeria he counted three more floors of opulent luxury, all of which was hidden behind the crumbling ruin he had seen from the outside.

Rumsfeld and Rove buried their fuzzy muzzles in the water of the fountain. A boy of thirteen came running out from a room somewhere to the side.

"Mucho! You are home!" he shouted, running to his older brother.

"Yes, Mucho, I have returned. Is mother here?"

Pig, of course, didn't understand this since it was all said in Babooban Arabic, but he caught the gist of it. The boy, Mucho, took the two asses and led them away towards where he had come from. The man, Mucho motioned for Pig to follow him as he stepped towards the huge wooden doors.

"Welcome to my home. You should say 'bismillah' now."

"Bismeelaw," Pig said dutifully.

"Good enough. I see you are surprised by the inside of my house compared with the outside. It is true, yes?"

Pig was grateful that the two parts of the question matched, allowing him to simply nod his head in the affirmative without too much undue thinking over which answer would be more appropriate.

"Here in Baboob, and especially in Turban, people shun displays of wealth because often, if the apple looks too delicious, it disappears from the tree. We don't try to make others feel inferior with displays of our wealth. The price of that is the evil eye and no good can come of it. Instead, we go to great lengths to hide our prosperity from those who don't need to see it. When you are invited inside, then, you are a guest and this is why upon entering a Babooban home, you should always say 'bismillah' which means 'in the name of Allah' and lets your host know that you don't suffer from envy or bring any evil intent.

"But the inside," Pig said, "It's so incredibly rich. I've been in some fancy places, but I've never felt such a sense of wealth. It seems a shame to let the outside fall apart. I mean, it would be so easy to fix that door, put a coat of paint..."

Mucho motioned for him to sit on one of the velvet cushions. "Take your shoes off before we go inside or my mother will skin you alive, guest or not." Then, "Don't you understand we want the outside to look as terrible as possible? We don't live outside, so, why should we waste our efforts for those who pass by on the streets to enjoy. Instead, we heap our luxury on the spaces we occupy. And besides, it's not as cheap as you think to make the outside look like that, in fact, it's very expensive." Mucho was unlacing his own boots as Pig sat and began to do the same.

"It's a funny thing about Turban, but the worse a house looks on the outside, the better you can know that the inside is. A very poor man's house might have a coat of paint on the outside while a rich man's – well – as you can see." He motioned expansively to the divine interior of his own family home. "My father, my brothers, my mother's brothers — we have all been successful in our smuggling and later in our trades. Come..."

Mucho pulled a pair of orange slippers with no heels from an alcove on the wall and handed them to Pig. He put a similar pair on his own bare feet.

"My shoes?" Pig asked.

"Oh, don't worry. Mucho or Fatima will take care of them. Come on."

Stepping into the large salon, Mucho led Pig to the second floor where six women in long skirts and peasant blouses moved around a traditional kitchen. They wore no veils or kaftans, only comfortable looking pajamas. A strong, handsome, grey haired woman with laugh lines around her eyes moved to Mucho and embraced him. Her blue eyes stood in contrast to her olive face, but that wasn't what surprised Pig.

Neither she, nor any of the other women in the kitchen were dressed like nuns! While Pig was taking in and enjoying everything else, he found himself outraged he had been lied to and misled into thinking Babooban women dressed like colorful nuns. His mind was seething but he didn't have time to consider the implications.

"Pigrone. This is my mother, Lalla Fatima." The woman grabbed Pig and stared into his face with a warmth and concern that unnerved him. It caused him to completely lose his train of thought and the feelings that went with it. She turned to Mucho and asked him several sharp questions in Arabic.

Mucho answered, then turned to Pig with a sheepish grin as the woman still held Pig by the shoulders, examining his face with concern. "She wanted to know how you did on the trail, she thinks you look too 'soft' to be a smuggler. I've told her you did well. I don't know if she believes me or not, but well, it's important to her."

Pig didn't understand at all. "But why should she care? I'm nothing to her." As he said it, Lalla Fatima apparently made up her mind and kissed Pig five times. Twice on each cheek and once on the forehead before releasing his shoulders and giving him her right hand.

The room was filled with soft murmurs of approval and feminine laughs at the look on Pig's confused face.

"Kiss her hand, idiot." Mucho whispered urgently.

Pig brought the woman's hand to his face and kissed it. He made what he hoped was a graceful bow. As fast as that, Lalla Fatima turned away from him and went back to ordering her daughters and servants about their work in the kitchen.

"Come on, they'll bring us breakfast in a few minutes." Mucho led him to the large downstairs saloon where they sat and put their feet up on cushioned stools.

"Mucho, can I take this handcuff off yet?" Pig asked, hoping that he would regain the full use of both hands. He was becoming used to the attaché, but it would be nice to be free of it. "I've done it. The case is here."

"Oh, no, not yet," Mucho told him. "You still need to deliver the case to Em-Mucho. We'll go after breakfast. I was hoping Fatima would be here, but apparently she has already gone to him."

"Lalla Fatima?" Pig asked.

Mucho gave him that look again. "Lalla Fatima is my mother. I meant my cousin Fatima."

"Oh," Pig said. Then, he remembered his outrage. "I thought all Babooban women wore the colorful nun outfits. None of those women in the kitchen were wearing anything like nun clothes. In fact, they didn't even look like they were Muslim with their heads uncovered, no veils, no burkas. Nothing."

Mucho laughed. "Why should they be covered when they are inside their own home? You have been invited here as a guest and will become a part of this family. There is no reason any of them should have put on their 'nun clothes' or be covered up in front of you."

Pig supposed it made sense. If he were a member of the family... hey, wait a minute. "What do you mean I'm going to be a member of

ORPHAN

HOLD
DO NOT SHIP

H1 – 000000000273

ISBN 9781939827319

CLIENT	Alternate Sourcing
STATION	TPP Receiving Station 03
HELD	2026 – 10 – 08 08:55

SHELF

If its order arrives, scan this label at a receiving station.

this family? No one told me anything about that. Is it because I joined you smuggling? Is it an honorary thing?"

Mucho smacked himself in the head. "Never mind. I wasn't supposed to say anything about it yet. Forget about it."

Pig didn't like the sound of that at all. "Mucho. You have to tell me now. What's going on?" Pig was trapped. He was on his own in a strange country, a strange city, the house of strangers, a strange land with strange customs and he suddenly knew for certain that he was in strange trouble too. "Tell me."

Mucho looked each way as if someone might be listening and then whispered, "You're going to marry Fatima."

Pig didn't have time to ask which Fatima he was going to marry since, at that moment, the girls came down the stairs bringing pancakes, honey, dates, walnuts, white cheese, olives, dried apricots, coffee, juice, and more food than Pig could imagine all of them together could eat in a week.

Em-Mucho

Mucho refused to answer any more of Pig's questions during breakfast. He stubbornly kept telling Pig to eat his food. The food was wonderful and Pig was hungry, but he was trying so hard to understand what was happening to him that he couldn't enjoy it. There were far too many questions that he needed to find the answers to.

All of the answers resided with Em-Mucho. He wanted to go right away, but Mucho and Lalla Fatima insisted that he keep eating. If his hands stopped for a moment or he didn't have a piece of food in them, the women (all of whom, by the way, were called Fatima), Mucho, and his brothers, (also named Mucho), would say “tkul, tkul, tkul.”

Mucho only spoke to him only once during the meal. “Tkul means eat. It's important that as a guest you don't leave hungry.”

By the time he managed to convince them he was not hungry, he was beyond full. He wondered if it would be impolite to make himself throw up in the bathroom, but wisely decided against it. At long last, Mucho moved to where their shoes had been neatly lined up and began to put on his boots. His younger brother brought a pack made from leather and carpet which he set on the floor.

The Fatimas cleaned up the mess from breakfast and then disappeared. “Am I going to marry one of them?” Pig asked – motioning towards the women.

Mucho snorted. “Don't be ridiculous. You've already seen their hair. I told you, you're going to marry Fatima.” Apparently, to Mucho the name sounded different than the name of every other Fatima Pig had met over breakfast. “Come on, he's waiting for us.”

Mucho hefted his pack and Pig, of course, carried the attaché he was attached to. He could hardly believe he was going to meet Sultan

Mucho al Mucho bin Mucho himself – Em-Mucho! He remembered the Contessa's bauble in his pocket. He would be able to deliver it!

As they walked through the narrow streets and alleyways of Turban, Pig saw ruins all around him. He wondered which rich family lived behind the crumbling facades and how the interiors might differ from that of Lalla Fatima's house.

Now that they were back in the streets, Pig was pleased to see that the women of Baboob really did dress like colorful nuns when they were outside their homes. His fantasies were grounded in reality, but all of the pleasure at that realization was subdued by the fact that apparently he had already been betrothed to whomever Fatima might be.

As he walked, he decided she must be an un-marryable woman. No Babooban man wanted her and so they were going to stage a shotgun wedding to marry off the ugly duckling of the family to Pig. All this way, all his dreams, everything he had hoped for — it was all going to end horribly. This was the real world, how could it end any other way for him.

The palace of Em-Mucho didn't have the ruinous facade of other wealthy homes. It was the richest place in Turban. There was no need to hide that. It was Em-Mucho's palace! High stone walls surrounded gardens where fruit trees laden with delicious treasures reached upwards to the heavens. A polished marble exterior greeted the supplicant as he came to beg the favors from the Sultan of Baboob. No pretense had been made that this was anything other than the home of the richest, most powerful, most favored personage in Turban or Baboob. As Pig took it in, he wondered if Em-Mucho was the richest man in all the world. It seemed likely.

For centuries, the stories of travelers who came to Baboob had been dismissed as myth. The gold window frames, the jewel studded banisters, the crystal windows, and the countless servants. Each tale had out-told the last but none of them came close to describing the true majesty of the Turbani Palace of Em-Mucho the Magnificent. Even during the twentieth century when photos and video footage had been smuggled out of the country, experts still dismissed the claims as far-fetched hoaxes. And yet, as he stood in front of the palace gates, Pig knew that the stories, if anything, had been undertolunder-toldd.

Armed guards asked Mucho his purpose. They sent a foot messenger running to the palace while continuing to eyeball them suspiciously. Pig saw a flit of powder blue inside the gardens from the corner of his right eye. When he turned to see it better, all he saw was the corner of a gown, disappearing into a doorway.

"Don't they already know you?" Pig asked Mucho. "Aren't you family?"

"Don't be silly," Much replied."Of course they know me and of course I'm family, but there is a way that things are to be done. They have to do their jobs just as we have to play our parts."

The messenger returned. The two men were led inside. Imagine the most fabulous gardens of the Arabian nights and you might have an idea of the magnificence they passed. Picture the palace of Aladdin or the riches of Sinbad, and you might be close to understanding the stately wealth of the building they were taken into. The cave of Ali Baba might have contained half the riches that stood before them as they were led into the throne room of Sultan Mucho al Mucho bin Mucho – Em-Mucho of Baboob. His throne stood empty. It was surrounded by priceless carpets, gold chalices, diamond pitchers, and a carved cedar box that overflowed with gold coins.

"Get down," Mucho said. He placed himself on his knees with his arms stretched before him and his forehead to the ground. Pig prostrated himself likewise. A blast of fanfare was blown through trumpets and a hush fell over the huge room. The echo of soft footsteps on carpet sounded like bullhorns because the silence of the room was so complete. And then, there was a giggle...

It was a madman's giggle. The giggle of a cracked person. The giggle of a person who had lost every bit of their sanity. It was the giggle of Em-Mucho. Pig wanted to look up, but dared not. He felt like Alice before the Queen of Hearts. All his other concerns disappeared as he realized that these could be his last moments on earth.

"Everyone out! Get out!" The madman screamed. Pig heard a rush as every foot in the room moved towards the door. He stood and ran, not daring to look at the holy personage of Em-Mucho who was yelling and screaming like a spoiled lunatic. A strong hand caught him and pulled him back.

"Not you, Pigrone!" The voice was deep and strong, not like the giggle or the scream. Em-Mucho spoke English. "You and my grand nephew will stay." It was Mucho who had grabbed him, not Em-Mucho, but the other Mucho we've already met. Pig saw the last of the uniformed Baboobans disappearing through the door and considered trying to escape and run towards it, but then, the door was closed. He stopped and turned slowly.

The man in front of him was the double of Master Mucho of the Pickle Juice Tea except for the golden crown tilted on his head. The same bent frame, the same beard, the same robe, the same knife – however there was something about his eyes, something different. Pig looked into the eyes of Em-Mucho but a sudden flash of light blue to his left caused him to turn.

Coming from behind the throne was the most incredible vision of loveliness Pig had ever seen. She was a goddess, a paragon of beauty, a wonder to behold like none that had ever walked the earth before her. Powder blue nun's habit with tall heeled brown boots showing underneath and yet, so small and perfectly shaped. Pig saw the perfect contours of breast and derriere. The dark brown eyes that stared at him from over the top of a light facial veil paralyzed him. He instantly became lost in my eyes...I mean...in her wonderful gorgeous exquisite almond shaped eyes.

"Ahem," Pig's attention was drawn back to Em-Mucho. "I believe my brother gave you something to bring to me?" Em-Mucho pointed at the attaché case.

"Darling Fatima," Em-Mucho said, "Get it please." Em-Mucho handed the vision of Pig's desire a golden key. She came towards him, never letting her eyes leave his. He held his hand out towards her with the attaché dangling from the attached handcuff.

Fatima grabbed his hand, unlocked the cuff, and allowed the attaché to fall to the soft carpet beneath it. Pig kept his hand extended as she knelt and picked up the case. She took it back to the waiting Em-Mucho.

Pig's hand rose as the weight of the case was released from it. He couldn't stop it.

"Put down your hand, idiot," Mucho whispered, "He's not Hitler." Pig quickly forced his hand back down.

“Peace and fair greetings upon you, my beloved Uncle, Sultan Mucho al Mucho bin Mucho of Baboob. I come before you with a trifle from my recent expedition. I also bring a new smuggler who seeks to win your favor, repay a debt, and earn his name.”

Mucho placed the backpack on the ground and undid its leather drawstring. From within he brought out a leather wrapped parcel. Fatima padded back down from the throne and took the package from Mucho's hands. She gave him a sly smile which despite her facial veil, was unmistakable in her brown eyes.

Em-Mucho looked at the two men. He certainly didn't look crazy. Pig wondered if the giggles and shrieks had belonged to someone else. Had they been an act or some sort of customary ritual?

“Peace and fair greetings to you, Smuggler and Smuggler Supplicant. I congratulate you on your journey and successful homecoming. First, I would see what my Grand Nephew has brought me this time.”

He gently unwrapped the leather from the parcel Fatima had taken to him. Inside was a leather bound book. The cover had been worked with tools and gold. Opening the pages, Em-Mucho gasped.

“This is the illustrated journal of Ibn Batuta! From where did you get this?”

“My Sultan and Honored Uncle – after the fall of Baghdad, many treasures were released into the world. It is my humble honor to have rescued but one to be preserved within your royal library, the greatest library in all the world.” Mucho bowed. Pig tried not to stare at Fatima who watched him from beside Em-Mucho.

Em-Mucho set the manuscript on a dark wooden table. He picked up the attaché case. “And, what has my lunatic brother sent me?” The case was facing away from Pig and so he didn't see the contents as Em-Mucho took the parcel from the case.

“Ah, yes, this is wonderful. Quite wonderful indeed.I needed this. And what of the man who brought it?” Em-Mucho turned his attention to Pig as he snapped the case shut. “What is your name?”

Pig was very grateful everyone was speaking English. “Your Excellency,” Pig started, not sure how to address Em-Mucho “My name is Pigrone Martin...”

"LIAR!!!" the madness was back in the face of Em-Mucho now. There was no doubt now that he was the giggler. "You dare to stand before me and lie to my face... to tell me a name that is not yours..."

Pig stepped back involuntarily. He was scared shitless. "I'm... I'm sorry, it's not really Pigrone, it's a nickname, I mean, Sire, your pardon, my name is really Martin...."

"Your name is Mucho!" Em-Mucho shouted at him. "You have walked the path of needles, carried the hidden, bypassed the deceived, and successfully fulfilled the blood oath. You are no longer a boy, no longer the man you once were, no longer the name you were once called. Now and forever, you are Mucho, son and smuggler of Baboob."

The madness was gone as quickly as it had come. Mucho who used to be called Pig, stood before the Sultan of Baboob as a new man. "What have you brought me," Em-Mucho asked.

Pig was confused. Em-Mucho had already taken the case. "Give him your smuggle gift," Mucho said to the brand new Mucho.

"But, I don't have a ...what's a smuggle gift?" Pig/Mucho asked.

Mucho hit himself in the forehead with the heel of his hand. "Nobody told you that you had to bring him a smuggle gift? For crying out loud..."

Fatima was desperately motioning to get Mucho/'Pig's attention. When he looked at her, she was patting herself on the side of her stomach. What in the world? What was she doing? Were they all insane?

Finally, Pig reached to the side of his own stomach and felt the bauble of the Contessa in his jacket pocket. How had Fatima known that was there?

"Your Holiness," Pig said, still unsure how to speak to Em-Mucho. " I bring this humble gift to you." Fatima was already in front of him nodding in approval and taking the red box which contained the precious bauble. She carried it to Em-Mucho.

The Sultan of Baboob opened the box and gasped in surprise.

"Extraordinary, Mucho," he said to Pig, who was still not at all used to the fact that he was no longer Pig but Mucho. "How did you get this? I thought to never see this again, lost in the passion of youthful folly. From where?"

Em-Mucho stopped. He looked at Pig-Mucho with even deeper scrutiny. “Did she give them to you too?”

Pig immediately understood what Em-Mucho asked him, but because Fatima (the most beautiful woman he had ever seen) stood beside Em-Mucho, he really didn't want to admit that, yes, the Contessa had given him the Royal Herpes. So he simply nodded.

The giggling again came and then “Magnificent, Mucho. Magnificent. You and I already connected in the most intimate of ways. You come carrying a precious gift I foolishly bestowed long ago never knowing that I would come face to face with it again. Something I long regretted losing and all while carrying something that was given and kept giving.”

“What is it?” the new Mucho Martin Hutchins asked. It came out of his mouth before he thought about how it might be inappropriate to ask.

“It is the symbol of my family, the crown jewel of all the crown jewels Baboob. This, my dear Mucho, is the very symbol of my position. This is the brooch of Hasan i-Sabah, the first Old Man of the Mountain, the founder of the Sultanate of Baboob and leader of the 'hashishan' assassins. Both this, and that other gift which she gave to you, came originally from him. You carry both the leaf and the herpes-simplex-two.”

Fatima and Mucho-Mucho, not Mucho-Martin-Hutchins-Pig, both watched with confusion. The royal herpes were a long held secret. Only Mucho-Pig and Em-Mucho knew what they were discussing. Not the bauble, which also had come back to Em-Mucho, but instead, the herpes. Em-Mucho continued to giggle.

Fatima cleared her throat. He kept giggling. She cleared her throat again. “Grandfather!” Em-Mucho turned towards her. Pig, truth be told, had barely taken his eyes from her.

“Oh, yes. I'm sorry, dear girl. I'd almost forgotten.”

“Mucho,” Em-Mucho said, looking at Pig. “We have a serious problem. I'm very pleased with your smuggle gift and with you, but I must unfortunately, address this issue. You cost my grand-daughter her job and I'd like to know what you plan to do about it.”

Pig-Mucho had no idea what Em-Mucho was talking about. “I'm sorry, but I've never seen her before today. I don't know how I could be responsible for...”

“Please excuse us for a moment,” Mucho said, dragging Pig a short distance away by the arm.

“Listen,” Mucho said , “I know none of this makes sense to you, but it's very serious. Your life is in danger. Fatima was the one who rescued you from the Secretary-of-the-Tunisian-Interior's house...”

“Kidnapped me, you mean. I told you, I was a guest,” Pig said indignantly.

“Well, as far as everyone else is concerned, she rescued you, so you better get that straight. Not only that, but, because she rescued you, she blew her cover as a house-girl and threw away years of work that had gotten her there.”

“I don't see how that's my fault,” Pig said.

“It doesn't matter what you see,” Mucho whispered to him. “The fact is, the grand-daughter of the Sultan sacrificed her position to save you and there are only two things that can be done when a Babooban woman loses her job.”

“What?” Pig asked.

“Well, the first thing is to kill the person responsible for the job loss,” Mucho said.

“Wait a minute. She rescued me — that's the stupidest thing I've ever heard. She rescued me and then she's going to kill me?”

“Good, I'm glad you've decided that she rescued you and yes, you're right, that would be stupid. The other thing, and the thing that pretty much everyone has decided on except you...” Mucho went on.

Pig thought he saw where Mucho was going. “I have to marry her.”

“Good,” Mucho slapped him on the back. “I'm glad you agree and understand.” He led Mucho-Pig back to Em-Mucho.

“Your Majesty Full of Grace,” Pig said, “ I beg your permission to marry this girl.”

“Granted on one condition,” Em-Mucho said, still looking at the bauble but then looking up at Fatima. “Will you marry this man or should we kill him?”

Fatima stood silently for a moment. She looked at Mucho-Pig-Martin-Dipshit and then she looked at the ceiling. She tapped her fingers together as if counting something. Then she looked back at her grandfather.

"We should probably kill him. He's deviant and a little bit stupid. I've followed him for a while now and he never noticed. Yes, let's kill him."

Em-Mucho looked sad. "Are you sure? I think he might have some potential? Seems a waste...."

Now she, Em-Mucho, and Mucho were all looking at Pig with sadness but they couldn't hold it when they saw the terror on his face and they all burst out laughing.

"Gotcha!" she said to Pig-Mucho and then turning to her grandfather said. "Of course, I'll marry this idiot. He's obviously lucky, like you said, he has some potential, and actually — I think he's cute. I've never had so much fun bagging someone and rolling them up in a rug."

Em-Mucho had stopped paying attention to her and was once more staring at the bauble... "Absolutely, astounding. I never thought I'd see this again..."

Epilogue

And that, dear readers, is the story of how I met my husband. It has been the perfect vehicle for introducing the world to the history, customs, and culture of the Sultanate of Baboob. Since I lost my job in Tunisia as a spy, my grandfather (Em-Mucho) appointed me as Royal Court Historian and Head of Public Relations and Marketing for the Sultanate. I persuaded him we needed to get the truth out about Baboob because there were so many lies and ruAnd that, dear readers, is the story of how I met my husband. It has been the perfect vehicle for introducing the world to the history, customs, and culture of the Sultanate of Baboob. Since I lost my job in Tunisia as a spy, my grandfather (Em-Mucho) appointed me as Royal Court Historian and Head of Public Relations and Marketing for the Sultanate. I convinced him we needed to get the truth out about Baboob because there were so many lies and rumors floating around the internet.

For those who are wondering what was in the attaché' case — that's another story. My grandfather made it a state secret. However, before I leave off writing this tale there are a few loose ends to tie up.

As I mentioned in the beginning, this story wasn't about Pig. The story revolved around a person called Pig who is really named Mucho. Pigrone was never Pig's name. His name was Martin, but people called him Dipshit. That slutty Contessa called him Pigrone and he was confused while everyone called him Pig because he hadn't yet learned his actual name is Mucho. By the way, it does sort of gross me out that he slept with a woman my grandfather slept with, but at least he didn't screw my grandma.

Let's be clear. My Mucho wasn't a hero when he started. He was a douchebag. He started as a boy (in a man's body), learned about the world, and discovered himself. Along the way, he fulfilled a rite of passage that turned him into my man. And I want to be really clear about something. He's not a douchebag any longer. If you say he is, I'll have to cut you...

Okay, I admit it, I call him Pig-Mucho sometimes and because I've been telling this story, I've started to think of him as Pig-Mucho. It's cute. He's cute and sort of pink. And he is my hero. Pig's education at ISHIT made him perfectly qualified to be the head of the 'Babooban School of English as a Foreign Language' at the University of Baboob. Em-Mucho created the position for him. Smugglers never pay taxes or repay student loans though so UNLV is out of luck for his loans.

Things were only beginning when Pig-Mucho arrived in Baboob. I'm sure you've read about the deal we made with Google. It's all over the internet. My favorite was the day they changed the Google logo to Babooble...but again, that's another story. It's impossible to tell you we lived happily 'ever' after because absolutes are almost always false, so, it's not very likely that this is...

THE END

Learn more about the Sultanate of Baboob and the mysteries of its violent and mysterious founder in Hasan i-Sabah — Volume Two of the Sultanate of Baboob Chronicles — available on Amazon and in fine bookstores everywhere.

About the Author

CD Damitio has spent the better part of three decades living, working, and wandering across four continents — from Morocco to Japan, Southeast Asia to the American West. He traded a TV and a VCR for a VW bus in 1996 and never quite looked back. His books cross genre lines the way he crosses borders: with curiosity, irreverence, and a stubborn refusal to settle for the official version of anything.

He is the founder of Baoism — a philosophy built around Bring Your Own Teachers, Bring Your Own Truth, and the radical idea that you are allowed to build your own world. Baoism is not a course, not a movement, and definitely not a guru product. It is a framework for people who are done waiting for permission. Explore it at Baoism.org.

His full catalog — fiction, memoir, philosophy, and everything in between — lives at Indignified.com/books. If you want to follow what he's thinking about, building, or arguing with himself over, find him on Xcrol.com/@cd, the privacy-first social network he built because the existing ones weren't worth the trade.

If you'd like to explore the characters in this book — along with the ways they cross over into all of CD Damitio's other work — head to The Sultanate of Baboob on W3WU.com. You'll find fan fiction, collaborations, character backstories, and threads that connect this world to everything else he has written.

W3WU.com is a collaborative worldbuilding platform built on a simple premise: the worlds inside great fiction belong to everyone who loves them. On W3WU, readers become co-creators. Writers share their IP openly and invite others in. Characters cross over. Stories branch. The result is something that resembles how mythology actually works — built by a community over time, bigger than any single author. It is, without exaggeration, the most interesting thing to happen to fiction since the printing press.